CW00518566

Lost in the Green Grass

Lost
in the
Green
Grass

- Henry Sands -

Matador
9 Priory Business Park,
Wistow Road, Kibworth Beauchamp,
Leicestershire. LE8 0RX
Tel: 0116 279 2299
Email: books@troubador.co.uk
Web: www.troubador.co.uk/matador
Twitter: @matadorbooks

ISBN 978 1838591 649

British Library Cataloguing in Publication Data.
A catalogue record for this book is available from the British Library.

Printed and bound in the UK by T J International, Padstow, Cornwall
Typeset in 11pt Minion Pro by Troubador Publishing Ltd, Leicester, UK

Matador is an imprint of Troubador Publishing Ltd

To my three lovable menaces:
Mr Digby, Django-Bear and Tilly.

- Chapter One -

Norfolk, England

It was at that moment that Lucinda, looking over the breakfast counter cluttered with newspapers and some cold, uneaten toast, knew that she was going to leave her husband, Anthony Palmer.

Anthony was sitting in his battered wooden chair, next to the back door of their 18th century Norfolk farmhouse, on the far side of the kitchen with his head buried in the weekend business supplement of *The Times*, oblivious to Lucinda's watchful gaze from the other side of the room.

After twenty-two years of marriage, this is what it had come to, Lucinda thought. Nothing. In the space where husband and wife were meant to have love and companionship, she felt only hollowness.

But for the first time for as long as she could remember, she felt excitement again. She drew this from the idea that there could be a way for this benign, lonely existence to finally come to an end.

It wasn't that she hated Anthony, or had become scornful towards him in the way some wives grew to despise their husbands. She thought him a decent man and often admired his perfect contentment in life. For Anthony was undeniably both decent and content. She just could not accept that this was it.

What a waste it seemed that her twilight years were to be spent watching her husband read the weekend magazine supplement in the kitchen, before raising his head now and again to make some innocuous comment that couldn't possibly interest either of them. For twenty-two years, she had politely nodded along to his murmurs with a, 'What's that, darling?' or sometimes, 'Yes, dear,' regardless of whatever the point being made was this time.

She had to remind herself she was fifty-eight, not eighty-five, increasingly frequently. Surely, there was still some excitement in life for her out there. She would regularly scour the internet reading blogs by middle-aged women who for one reason or another had packed in their lives and gone travelling. She had read *Eat, Pray, Love* multiple times, regularly envisaging herself as the protagonist, Liz Gilbert. A summer spent learning to paint in Tuscany or visiting archaeological ruins, before rolling around in the sand and having a one-night stand with a mysterious and handsome young man didn't sound too bad at all.

It wasn't even the idea of romance that she wanted; she hadn't been sexual with Anthony for many years. Christ, she thought, she wasn't even sure her body would know what to do anymore. But she longed for something unexpected and spontaneous.

Lucinda and Anthony used to be quite a social couple. Norfolk, she felt, was good for that, with plenty of dinner parties taking place every night of the week. She had always put the convivial nature of the county down to its location; it being far enough away from London meant that daily commuting to the city wasn't really an option, and therefore everyone lived as if they were *expatriates*.

But the drinks parties and dinners that had once filled their diaries had gradually declined over the years. At first, Lucinda put it down to people getting a bit older and so entertaining less, but after a girls' lunch a few years ago that had flowed with a touch too much white Burgundy, a close friend had revealed something that Lucinda had already suspected, deep down. Her friends' husbands had grown rather, well, just a bit bored of Anthony and his seeming unwillingness to make an effort to strike interesting conversation.

Not that Anthony himself would have minded at all about being branded antisocial, really. He was happy enough just pottering around making himself busy at home. An ideal morning for him would have been attentively following an instruction manual line by line, preferably one he had ordered in especially, having lost the original, and using it to fix a broken washing machine. Bleeding all the radiators in the house for the umpteenth time that month was another good option. 'Always good to be sure,' he would mutter.

For many years, Anthony had been a partner in a small accountancy firm, ADR Advisors, based in London and which specialised in looking after the accounts for small and medium-sized companies, as well as individuals' tax returns. Anthony had been the fourth partner there, but the three founders decided not to extend the name to ADRP, with the view their own three initials were quite enough. True to form, the Palmer contingent hadn't put up much resistance and seemed perfectly happy maintaining the status quo.

Several years later, ADR Advisors was bought by a bigger firm and, in order for Anthony to secure a reasonable payment as part of the sale, he was to continue to act as a senior adviser to the new firm, Chapman Parker.

The new set-up had only required him to be in the office for three days a week, and the general expectation was that he would gradually scale back his workload further over time. Having cut down to just one day a week, though, he realised how much he missed the routine and the backbone that the working structure had instilled in his life, and so, to the bafflement of the more junior members of staff, he quickly upped his voluntary attendance to three days a week.

On Tuesday mornings, Lucinda would drop him at Downham Market station, in time for the 07.21 train. This would normally get him into the Chapman Parker office in Chancery Lane by 09.30. He had a small flat that had once belonged to his mother in Victoria, off Vincent Square, where he stayed on Tuesday and Wednesday evenings, before taking the train back to Norfolk at 16.48 from Kings Cross on a Thursday.

His three-day week in the office had earned him a rather ambiguous nickname amongst the same group of junior employees: TWAT. Rarely for Anthony, he looked almost angry on being addressed in such a manner by this year's summer intern, before the second-year university student quickly pointed out that the term reflected his attendance in the office only on Tuesdays, Wednesdays And Thursdays. If truth be told, the title took some getting used to, but although perhaps lacking in overt warmth, the perceived office camaraderie that Anthony felt was generated as a result was sufficient enough to enable him to decline regular office drinks and other social events, and so was worth putting up with.

Lucinda often wondered how it was that she was more bored and lonely when Anthony was back at the house in Norfolk than when he was away in London, but it was undeniably the case. At least when it was just her at Ferryman's Cottage, she felt she had space. She had her own privacy. But when Anthony was at home, it was his constant shadow of apathy that depressed her so. And that's how she self-diagnosed her state of mind: depression.

Of course, she had thought about leaving Anthony before. In her imagination, her new life was full of unexpected twists, turns and impromptu excitement. The truth, though, was that she knew she didn't really have anywhere to go, nor many savings left to fund her escape. The money she had was largely tied up in their house and the grazing land their house backed onto, which they had since purchased separately. Though, technically, that was Anthony's money.

In the past, when she'd had these visions of her new life, the initial excitement hadn't taken long to dissipate as she inevitably came back to the conclusion that she was just being silly, and there was no way it was a viable plan. Instead, it made much more sense for her to just continue ploughing on as they were, attempting to make the life they had a little more fulfilling. These attempts were initiated with gusto for several days, sometimes weeks, before she felt unable to carry the weight of Anthony's detachment, and the whole cycle started once again.

But this Saturday morning, it was different. She knew as she watched her husband of the last two decades that things were going to change. This time, it was for real, and she *was* going to leave him, once and for all. Her fantasies had been going on long enough now, and it was time to make them a reality. From somewhere inside herself, where previously the conviction to go through with it had been found wanting, she now found determination and a core of inner strength. Yes, she would leave him. But not just yet. It was the last weekend of November, and with Christmas on the horizon, plans had already been made for her children, Sophie and Jack, to come and stay. She would get through December, quietly planning the details of her escape, and be on her way in early January. New year, new start.

The mere thought of her life ahead liberated her from the shackles of the repetitive and mundane existence she felt she lived, and gave her an additional spring in her step as she headed upstairs, leaving Anthony to his newspaper in the kitchen.

*

It hadn't always been like this with Anthony. But then again, it had hardly been a relationship that had developed from raw passion.

Lucinda had been married before, to a man she loved desperately and who loved her back. David Morley.

Lucinda and David had first met as teenagers at a mutual friend's 18th birthday party, in a barn in Hampshire when, after a few too many glasses of wine, Lucinda had woken up next to him in an empty stable.

Most of their clothes were lying scattered around the stable floor and, given the lack of conventional bedding available – it had most certainly not been the intention of the host's mother for guests to be sleeping in the stable – they had instead covered themselves in hay, which provided a surprising amount of warmth if not comfort.

The next morning, they scarpered before the lifeless limbs of sleeping bodies, scattered around the main barn and in tents next to the parked cars, arose.

David dropped her at Winchester train station the next morning in his father's old Jaguar E-Type convertible that he had borrowed for the drive down from his family home in Rutland. During the drive, he had rested his hand on her lap intermittently. The whole experience made Lucinda feel incredibly grown up. At the station, he leant over and kissed her once more, before telling her that he hoped he might be able to see her again soon. She hoped so too.

In fact, she didn't see him again for six years. During that time, she had briefly gone to Chelsea Arts School, but dropped out on realising – thanks to some painfully unsubtle reports from her tutor, sometimes in front of the rest of the class – that she wasn't, in fact, very good at art. With her confidence crushed, she began working for Savills in the Notting Hill office instead, quickly working her way up the hierarchy thanks to her charm and relentless energy, and her confidence ratcheted back up along with her sales figures and popularity within the team.

Lucinda often wondered what had become of David Morley, particularly after a string of uninspiring dates, and would regularly reminisce to herself about their night of frolicking in the stable. Then, six years later, almost exactly to the day, she finally found out. By chance, he walked right into her Savills office, enquiring with his self-assured charm that she remembered so clearly about a mews house they were selling just off Holland Park Avenue. Lucinda politely asked if he was already registered with the estate agent, using the opportunity to quickly check their client folders, and read that he was now an associate at a boutique macro hedge fund based just off Grosvenor Square, and making quite a name for himself in that world as an up-and-coming star of the future.

Lucinda grabbed the keys to the house from her colleague's desk, who, rather fortuitously she felt, just happened to have popped out of the office at that moment to grab some lunch. With her most beguiling smile, which had become something of an office phenomenon, Lucinda offered to show David around the mews house herself.

She had recognised him immediately but said nothing, wondering if he would remember her from their summer's night. In fact, he had instantly noticed her face on stepping into the office, but couldn't place it until they were halfway through the tour. At that point, they both broke out into childish smiles and agreed a date to go for a drink the following week at the nearby Ladbroke Arms.

They were inseparable from that moment. Lucinda moved into David's newly purchased mews house four months later, and they married the following spring, at St John's Church, off Ladbroke Grove, just around the corner from their house.

After two years of marriage, their daughter, Sophie, was born. When Lucinda became pregnant again the following year, 32 Ladbroke Walk was starting to look a bit small. They decided to make a plan to move to Hampshire, to an Elizabethan rectory on the edge of the small village of Itchen Abbas, which had recently come on the market.

David had an older brother, Mark, who was to inherit the family house in Rutland. He didn't much fancy the idea of being the younger brother parked down the road, waiting for handouts like a grateful Labrador under the kitchen table. Hampshire gave them their own space, liberated from the scrutiny David had in Rutland that came with being Lord Higglestone's second son.

Lucinda was confident she would be able to negotiate a switch from Savills in Notting Hill to their Winchester office fairly easily, and David was happy to start commuting on the train four days a week, given that he already worked from home most Fridays anyway. They agreed it was a perfect set-up, and although Lucinda felt sad at the prospect of selling Ladbroke Walk, which she associated with David's return into her life, she knew it was time for the next chapter. Each morning as she woke up next to David, normally resting her head on his surprisingly unhairy chest, she didn't once take for granted just how blissfully happy she was.

*

When the phone rang for Lucinda that Thursday afternoon, she couldn't comprehend the devastating magnitude of what was being said. That was probably as much to do with the professional, level tone of Alfred's voice on the other end of the phone, as her own state of denial.

Alfred was the long-standing porter from Boodles, David's club, where he had been having lunch that day with Johnny, an old school friend who Lucinda had never quite taken to.

'Mrs Morley, you're needed at St Thomas' Hospital immediately. It's David.' Despite the urgent words, Alfred possessed a measured calmness in his voice, which you could be confident would not change regardless of whether he was announcing a birth, death or resurrection. But on this occasion, even by his standards as a stickler, his voice wavered slightly as he uttered the name of one of his favourite of the younger members at Boodles.

Moments earlier, he had watched David stride out of the club after a good lunch, a "two bottler". It was only a matter of seconds before a delivery truck then sped around the corner from Jermyn Street. The driver was looking to his right, ensuring there was no traffic swinging down off Piccadilly, and failed to see the young gentleman step out on the street in front of him. The driver heard the unmistakable sound of impact and a sternum crunching, before the high-pitched scream of a woman on the pavement watching the scene confirmed his worse fears.

At eight months pregnant, it wasn't easy for Lucinda to get anywhere quickly, but she packed up her desk in the Savills office, for she had not yet taken her maternity leave, and hailed a black cab from Holland Park Avenue. Twenty minutes later, she arrived at St Thomas' Hospital.

Still more curious than concerned by the call, she was surprised to find a nurse looking pensive waiting for her at the entrance to the hospital.

'Mrs Morley? Please, come this way,' the nurse said, and escorted her in silence to an office where a doctor and two surgeons were waiting with solemn expressions.

'There isn't much time, I'm afraid, Mrs Morley,' the doctor said before opening a door. There, lying on a bed with tubes coming out of his nose, and bloodied bandages around his head and torso, was David.

He smiled at her, like he always did, the same way he had smiled at her when he dropped her off at the train station all those years ago. Lucinda was shocked. This was the last thing she had expected. David used what little strength he had left to put his left hand on Lucinda's pregnant stomach.

She held his face. 'I'm so sorry,' he whispered. 'Completely bloody daft.'

And those were his last words.

Moments later, the machines stopped bleeping, and David's eyes shut for the last time. And that was that. With a two-year-old child and another expected in less than a month, Lucinda was a widow at just twenty-seven.

*

With the support of her family, and some money that had been set aside for her from David's trust, Lucinda was managing with Sophie and Jack okay in Ladbroke Walk. Their move to Hampshire no longer made sense, and she pulled out of the sale and took Ladbroke Walk off the market.

Her mother would visit twice a week and look after the children, giving her at least a little time for herself, a rare indulgence since Jack had been born.

Just when she thought her life was as happy as it could be, the rug had been pulled out from under her feet, and her life had been turned on its head.

She missed her friends, and she missed her job too and the little insights into the lives of all her customers that came with it. But most of all, she missed David. Enormously.

Each day, she forced herself to be strong and crack on with the duties in hand, doing everything she could to give Sophie and Jack the happiest childhood possible. For that's what David would have wanted her to do. And although she was both surprised and relieved at just how well she was coping, each morning when she woke up in their marital bed without him, she was reminded of her loss and the heartache she had suppressed before the day started all over again.

As the children grew up and became more restless, Lucinda found it harder and harder to manage them in London, what with their different after-school engagements and weekend sports clubs. Her mother was still driving down for two days a week from Norfolk to help her, and she had an au pair to pick up Sophie from school on another two, but she still struggled without the support of her husband to help.

She still dreamt of living in a farmhouse, with her children growing up and running around in the open countryside, and having a similar rural upbringing to the one that she and her sister had so enjoyed. Hampshire no longer made any sense at all, though. David had only wanted to move there precisely because he knew so few people there. Now Lucinda needed all of the support and companionship that she could get.

She knew her friends had concerns over her leaving London as a young widow. But, having endured two years of acquaintances trying to arrange blind dates and issuing supposedly random dinner invitations with questionable other singletons, Lucinda was comfortable in the knowledge that she was never going to replace David. She therefore felt no inclination to try to do so. What she had was irreplaceable, and she had grown to be content with that.

With Sophie turning six and Jack nearly four now, Lucinda packed up Ladbroke Walk for the last time and moved to Ferryman's Cottage, which, despite the modesty of its name, was a gracious four-bedroom Georgian house with beautiful proportions typical of the era, and much more space. It was made available from a nearby estate, the owner of which was a friend of Lucinda's parents, who had decently let them know it was soon to be available as an injection of cash was needed to sure up some of the other properties on the estate.

The house was positioned on the edge of the village of Castle Acre, a pretty and originally Norman settlement in West Norfolk, and overlooked the church green.

It also had a small garden, which opened up onto nearby farmland. And as a Savills brochure might have read, it boasted a beautiful view of the Nar Valley as well as a chalk stream popular with local anglers flowing gently down through its lush green banks.

Conveniently, it was also only ten minutes down the road from where Lucinda had grown up and where her parents still lived. Being a single mother living down the road from her parents was far from what she had expected from life; any concerns she had had about having her mother now living on top of her were far outweighed by the additional childcare support she now had at her disposal.

*

She had met Anthony Palmer at Fakenham Racecourse on New Year's Day, six months after moving back to Norfolk.

Lucinda had taken Sophie and Jack, along with some friends and their children, as it was one of the most popular social events of the year for everyone to get together and forget about their hangovers from the night before.

A large group of family friends were having drinks on the edge of the pavilion next to the finish line of the track, when she noticed Anthony standing slightly awkwardly on the edge of a conversation with Lucinda's cousin, Charlie.

He was probably a little older than Lucinda, though well dressed, and he looked, well, likeable. Lucinda joined the conversation and soon found herself speaking to him alone.

Anthony hadn't been married before, not that it seemed to bother him. He lived a quiet, straightforward life, living in a small three-bedroom terraced house on Rowena Crescent in Battersea. He'd been up in Norfolk for New Year, visiting one of his old Oxford friends who had married a local girl, having received a fairly last-minute invitation after his hosts realised they were short on men for the evening.

Lucinda hadn't thought that much about trying to find a new husband since she'd moved to Norfolk. When she left London, she left with the full intention of a quiet single life – perhaps getting back into painting if she ever had the time – but she had been surprised by the loneliness she felt, particularly when the days drew shorter. This contrasted with London life, when even if she hadn't been busy herself, the buzz of everything going on around her created an impression of purpose. At Ferryman's Cottage, once the children had gone to bed, there was no noise. Just silence; and she found herself spending many nights looking at the bright stars above and reading.

She was also becoming increasingly aware of the rate at which her finances were depleting. With much of the money from the sale of Ladbroke Walk being locked up in trusts for Sophie and Jack, which they gained access to when they reached their 21st birthdays, as it had come from David's family trust in the first place, there wasn't all that much left over. Having left her job to look after the children and with no income, she was conscious of finances for the first time in her life.

Unlike so many of the men that she had been set up with since David died, Anthony was altogether a rather different kettle of fish. An anomaly.

Friends had understandably, but wrongly, assumed that the sort of man Lucinda would be looking for would be almost a like-for-like replacement for David. What they failed to comprehend was that, in Lucinda's eyes at least, her charming, considerate, vivacious David was always going to be irreplaceable. So why, she thought, try?

Anthony was steady, reliable and sufficiently financially stable to cover the costs of their lives, including the school fees for Sophie and Jack. That would do, wouldn't it? Lucinda knew she had found the best man she could have hoped for with her first marriage, which had been driven entirely by the passion of the heart. This time around, she just needed stability. And Anthony offered that.

And so, after less than nine months of weekend visits to Ferryman's Cottage, during which time Anthony had managed to strike up a firm fondness for the children, and they for him, who they called "Ant-Ant", their engagement was announced. The news was received with full understanding and support, if not euphoria, from their broad circle of friends, both in London and Norfolk.

*

What would happen to Ferryman's Cottage once she had left? Lucinda wondered to herself. Although she had been the one who originally bought it, Anthony technically now owned most of it if you calculated the mortgage repayments. And that was before considering the additional 22 acres of land Anthony purchased outright from the local farmer, Jon Mason, when he needed a cash injection after his experiment with a new exotic sugar replacement crop backfired dramatically, leaving him nothing to harvest at all for one full year.

From her bedroom window, she could see through to the kitchen below, where in the corner of her eye she was aware of Anthony still slumped in his chair. But she wasted no energy setting her eyes on him. Instead, she looked out beyond the kitchen, out over her back garden and down towards the River Nar below that flowed more heavily in the winter months.

Lucinda had a huge attachment to Ferryman's Cottage. After all, she had moved in when she had been at her most vulnerable, and had somehow managed to build a new life there. She would love to be able to include the house in her future plans, but as she plotted her escape, she was realistic about the fact that she would likely need to sell the house to raise some much-needed cash to fund her adventures, whatever they might be.

Her family time at Ferryman's Cottage had nothing but fun memories for her, from Sophie's weekend sleepovers with young teenage school friends to Jack's erotic vampire-themed 18th birthday party, which amusingly led to much concern amongst the neighbours that a sexually devious death cult had arrived in their sleepy Norfolk village.

But since Sophie and Jack had headed off to university, their visits home had, as to be expected, become much less regular, and they had fewer houseguests than ever. They didn't really need the space, though it had certainly helped enable her and Anthony to live the independent lives that they had increasingly become used to. Perhaps it had been the reason why the marriage had lasted this long. 'There are few things that can't be fixed through the protection of personal space,' her friends would regularly remind her if she spoke of her marital boredom. No, she would look back fondly on the time they'd had there.

Lucinda had devised her plan. This Christmas, she would make even more effort than before to make sure it was a happy, joyful occasion, particularly for Sophie and Jack. She would be careful not to reveal her plans to anyone throughout the holidays, and then quietly and without fuss, once Sophie had returned back to Scotland and Jack to London, she would purchase her plane tickets and commence her adventure. She was unsure yet of exactly where she was going to go, but just the knowledge that her life was about to change, after what had felt to her like twenty-two years of numbness, brought a smile to her face.

- Chapter Two -

Tulum, Mexico

Jack's senses were in overdrive as the Mexican hash seeped into his bloodstream. It was 6pm and he was leaning back on a bamboo mat on the beach next to the bar at Camp Mayo, the luxury campsite where he was working. The DJ had just started his sundown set.

Chilled electronic music filled the air around him as the gentle waves from the warm Caribbean Sea splashed his feet.

Jack had been in Tulum for five weeks now. He had originally planned to spend two months travelling across the country, starting in Tulum before finishing up in Cabo on the far west side of Mexico before heading home and starting his new job as a junior property surveyor at Brennan & Co, the upmarket commercial real estate business based in Marylebone. He found, though, that having spent a week by the Caribbean Sea, he couldn't quite bring himself to leave, and made an executive decision to scrap the rest of the trip and stay put for the rest of his time in Mexico. Jack had always been one for sticking to something once he liked it, and he very much liked Tulum.

He had met Leonardo on one of his first evenings in Tulum as he took a sunset stroll along the sand and stumbled across a meditation class taking place around a campfire on the beach. Originally from New York, Leonardo, who was ten years older than Jack, had arrived in Tulum five years ago after deciding he no longer wanted to run nightclubs for the rich and famous in New York.

He set up a small, trendy camp of twelve yurts close to the Mayan Ruins, capitalising upon the rising popularity of the luxury eco-glamping scene. Using his experience from the world of high-end nightclubs, Leonardo knew how to create a marketable environment for wealthy Americans wanting to play the comfortable hippy for a few days before returning to their corporate jobs. He had effectively created Camp Mayo as a permanent boutique festival for its guests, with yoga and classes in spiritual awakening during the day, before transitioning to sunset dance parties on the beach, and where a liberal approach to both sex and drugs was encouraged.

When Jack first arrived in Tulum, he had been staying in a small beach hut for $40 a night further down the beach. Leonardo needed an extra pair of hands helping with the day-to-day running of Camp Mayo, managing guests and occasional extra support on the music decks, and Jack leapt at the chance. He thought it best not to mention that he didn't actually have any experience as a DJ, and was confident that through his Spotify account he'd be able to find some pretty reasonable pre-mixed sets, leaving him to twist the balance and fade nozzles on occasion to give the impression of someone who knew what they were doing. Besides, at Camp Mayo, most of the guests didn't want anything too specialised; some standard trippy trance vibes, starting gently while the sun went down before increasing the pace and intensity as the night drew on, worked ideally for them.

On this particular evening, it was Diego who was DJing to the crowd of forty-odd swimwear-clad tourists, watching the sun going down. Unlike Jack, Diego really did know what he was doing and was widely considered to be the number one DJ in Tulum for that season. He was a friend of Leonardo, so he would occasionally come and play at the Camp when he wanted to test out new material ahead of his two big nights a week. They were held at Casa Jaguar on Thursdays, a chic Argentinian restaurant and club in the town, and at Papaya Playa Project on Saturdays, a large beachfront bar at the far end of the beach.

Jack lay back on the sand and closed his eyes. There was something about smoking hash that made everything feel so much better, he thought. Every sense he had would become immeasurably heightened. The music developed a hypnotic rhythm, food would taste delectable and even sex gained an indescribable intensity. He was feeling pretty good.

With a Corona in one hand, Jack sat up and stared out to sea, thinking about his life. At moments like this, he would often think about his father. Although he had died just a few weeks before he was born, Jack felt he had a pretty good idea of what his father was like. He suspected this image of him stemmed from photographs and the stories his mother and others had recounted to him over years. Although he was fond of Anthony, and always appreciated the way he had been a support for his mother, that didn't stop him wondering what life would have been like had his father not had his accident.

Jack relit his now extinguished joint and inhaled deeply, holding it in his lungs for as long as was comfortable. He was not a habitual smoker but had enjoyed it occasionally in the past, though in Tulum, he'd certainly increased his intake. He knew about the perceived risks and his mother's claims that it would fry his brains, but Jack was becoming adamant that his brain worked best, in fact, *after* he had been smoking. He could put his mind to any subject, issue or being and would be able to provide himself with a depth of analysis and thought that he would rarely be able to conjure up otherwise.

At that moment, his laser focus directed his thoughts towards the impossibly perfect curves of a young brunette girl's bottom as she danced a few yards away on the edge of the sea. Wearing very tight denim shorts and a shell-stitched green bikini top, he guessed the girl was about twenty-two. The inevitable impact gravity would one day have on her ample bust remained far into the future.

The girl was dancing with her hands twisting up in the air, pushing them through her long brown hair as she swung her head from side to side and moved her body to the tribal beats of the music that was gradually increasing in pace and volume.

He half wondered if Diego had spotted her dancing too and was purposely increasing the intensity of the music to watch her body respond, as if he was operating her limbs like a puppet on strings; only his strings were the beats of the tunes.

With Leonardo being the only other possible contender, Diego had had more flings with Tulum's most beautiful women than anyone else in the area. Being the top DJ on the strip, performing at the two biggest nights of the week, meant that everyone knew Diego. And every woman – as well as a good handful of men – wanted to go to bed with him at the end of the night. Diego knew the power his music gave him. He knew that the cocktail of dancing, pheromones, alcohol and drugs amongst such an attractive group of people more often than not led to one thing: sex. He knew no one was more appealing to people dancing away than he was, fuelling their night with his jungle beats. Jack admitted that Diego was probably right about that; but he also knew that the woman he had set his eyes on that late afternoon, dancing away in front of him, was a woman that he wanted for himself.

Gesturing to Simmy, the barman, he had a couple of margaritas made up and walked over to introduce himself to the girl in green. The rich flavours of the fruit in the cocktail, mixed with the salt-dusted rim of the glass, were a wonderful tonic for his now hyper-exaggerated tastebuds.

Jack introduced himself and handed the girl one of the margaritas. Her name was Makenna, and she had joined three of her friends in Tulum for a week's holiday following their final exams at the University of South California, just outside LA.

With a striking jawline and dark, penetrating eyes, there was something beguiling about Makenna which immediately infatuated Jack. They spoke and danced with each other for about half an hour, before the sun had completely disappeared. Diego was winding his set down, and people started heading back to their hotels to get ready for dinner and the night ahead. Jack took the opportunity to persuade Makenna to join him for an early supper at a little beach bar, a leisurely five-minute walk further up the beach.

At the bar they were given a table in what resembled a giant bird's nest made from rattan, with some cushions to sit on and a hurricane lantern for light. The wind swung the nest gently, reinforcing their enclosed privacy. The waiter brought them a sharing plate of fish tacos and a couple of rum-based house cocktails. Three hours later, they were both pleasurably intoxicated.

Jack suggested linking back up with her friends and going on somewhere in town, but at that point, Makenna moved her resting hand from Jack's knee, up his inner thigh and onto his now increasingly hard cock.

'Why don't we head back to your fancy yurt you keep telling me about?' Makenna asked softly.

Jack ordered the bill, after which they made their way back to the beach. Although it was night, the brightness of the stars above and the illuminated plankton glowing along the breaking shoreline ahead of them provided the perfect balance of light; enough to be able to see where they were going, but not too much to stand out visibly to any other late-night walkers.

Jack found himself wondering what state he had left his yurt in that afternoon before heading out, desperately hoping it wasn't such a disgrace as to put off Makenna on arrival. He had learnt that there was nothing women find less appealing than having sex with someone they've just met amongst a seabed of empty beer cans, dirty clothes and an overflowing bin with last night's supper still festering at the bottom of it.

In the end, he needn't have worried about what he may or may not have left out, as well before they reached the yurt, Makenna stopped and began stripping off her clothes. First, her little t-shirt and bikini top came straight over her head and dropped to the floor, revealing what Jack felt were frankly gargantuan breasts, given the petiteness of the rest of her body.

Her little denim shorts followed, revealing just the tight green thong-like bikini bottoms she had been wearing. They were held up by a bow on each side with a drawstring. Makenna pulled the drawstring and the bikini bottoms came apart in two pieces and fell to the ground. For a split second she stood there, and Jack was mesmerised. She was the most perfect physical specimen he had ever set his eyes on. And she was here, standing naked in front of him.

The moment of silence was swiftly broken as Makenna turned towards the sea and said, 'C'mon, Jack, race me in,' and with that she turned and ran towards the breaking waves in front of them.

Jack, still not quite believing his luck, removed his clothes as quickly as he was able to, while getting one foot caught up in his shorts, nearly causing him to fall over. Finally, he was clear and running towards the sea to catch up with Makenna, who was already through the first break of waves.

As the Caribbean Sea remained shallow for further than Jack expected, by the time he reached Makenna, he could still keep his feet firmly on the sandy seabed beneath him. This was fortuitous because no sooner had he reached her than she jumped towards him, wrapping her arms around him and kissed him again, this time even more energetically than before. Using the sandbank beneath her, she kicked herself off the ground and straddled her legs around Jack's waist. With her left hand, she reached down and firmly clasped Jack's now heavily swollen cock.

Her hand worked its way up and down Jack's shaft a couple of times, before she manoeuvred all of him inside her. Throwing her head back to look at the stars, Jack pulled her hips down, thrusting his cock as deep into her as he could go.

Her weightlessness in the water enabled Jack to control the movement of her body in a way he knew he would never have been strong enough to do onshore, and he intended to make the most of it.

In the distance, they could just hear the faint sounds of a jungle music beat starting over the sound of the waves around them. As Jack felt himself getting closer to climaxing, Makenna threw her head forward again and whispered into his ear, 'Come with me.' A few moments later, they let go of their tangled embrace and fell backwards into the warm water.

They swam back towards the beach and gathered up their clothes. Jack handed his shirt for Makenna to use as a towel, before drying himself off with it. Once both were dressed, they lay down on the dunes behind them in silence, Jack with his arm around her, and looked up to watch the stars.

Jack closed his eyes, with Makenna's head resting on his chest. He soon drifted off to sleep.

*

When Jack was woken a few hours later by the rising sun, Makenna had gone. In his pocket he saw a folded receipt, on the back of which was written, *That was a wonderful evening. M x*

At first, Jack was taken aback by her sudden departure, before he smiled. *What a cool girl*, he thought to himself. These American girls knew how to enjoy themselves.

Inside his jeans pocket was his phone, which had eight new WhatsApp messages from the group chat, *Tainted-in-Tulum*, which he shared with Leonardo, Diego and a few other friends working there.

The messages were mostly updating each other with the various goings-on in town, along with a selection of photos from amusing scenarios of holidaymakers they had come across. These were normally of individuals in compromising situations, including one of a couple seen the night before riding their rented cruiser bicycles completely naked down the main strip of the town.

Jack laughed and made his way back to his yurt. He knew they had new arrivals coming that day that needed welcoming.

- Chapter Three -

Norfolk, England

Diana McAlpine's shooting weekend two weeks before Christmas had been in Lucinda's calendar since late June. While many of Lucinda's friends had stopped asking them to social events, Diana's invitations inevitably, and loyally, continued to arrive.

Since Diana's husband, Charlie, had died three years ago unexpectedly from a heart attack, aged sixty-four, Lucinda had grown close to Diana, and the two women tried to meet for coffee mornings at a boutique hotel in nearby Swaffham every other week.

Lucinda noticed that some women retreat into themselves when they lose their husbands, choosing to save the memories they had rather than seeking new ones, but Diana was the opposite. Her husband had been a larger-than-life character who was always the last to leave any party. Being the centre of attention that he so often was meant Diana had rather taken a back seat. Since his untimely death, she had thrown herself into social life more than anyone else Lucinda knew. But in one of the few moments Diana had let her guard down, she confessed to Lucinda that the main reason she kept herself so busy was actually because it distracted her from thinking too much about Charlie, who she missed desperately.

His premature death meant that not only had Diana lost her husband of thirty-two years, but also brought about the end of her time living at Bickham Hall, a fine Jacobean house surrounded by rolling parkland and a 3,000-acre farm that her husband had inherited soon after they married.

Her eldest son, Hugo, had packed in his job in the city and moved his young family up from the house they had only recently moved to in West London to take over the Hall and farm.

A separate farmhouse on the estate had been converted for Diana which, while perfectly comfortable and tucked away in one of Norfolk's few small valleys, was quite a transition from running the large household she had become used to.

Hugo had made many changes to the running of the farm since he had taken over. Aside from the shoot, of course, which was already one of the finest partridge shoots in the county and had clearly been a primary area of focus for Charlie and his trusty gamekeeper, Tommy. This was at the expense of what he deemed to be overly extravagant modern-day expenditure, such as heating the house outside of arctic conditions or replacing the temperamental Aga, despite Diana's protestations at never having managed to have served the Christmas turkey before 9pm.

In order to ensure that his mother still felt involved in the house, on moving in, Hugo encouraged her to co-host a shooting weekend with him each year, to which she invited most of his late father's best friends.

The reality was that these weekends were as much to keep his mother busy as to have an opportunity to see his father's old friends, who never declined an invitation to spend a day in the company of the next generation of "scoundrels".

Lucinda admired Diana and loved her generous and lively weekends, but as much as she was looking forward to this year's event, there was a part of her that now dreaded the prospect of dragging Anthony along in tow, given the circumstances. Not exactly the consummate sportsman, Lucinda could happily laugh off his rather imprecise shooting, but she hadn't got used to his complete lack of ability or appetite to socialise normally with the other husbands. This was half the reason she didn't mind that their invitations had dried up, but she was damn well going to grin and bear any embarrassment that might arise on Diana's weekend, which was always jolly, and an admirable example of making the most out of whatever life threw at you.

*

After lunch, the women decided to leave the men to their own devices for the final drive and walk back along the River Stiffkey towards Diana's house.

The sun was out, and the reflection of the hedgerows glistened in the water. Norfolk looked beautiful in the soft light, with endless skies above them that reminded her of the Kenyan plains. Diana dropped back slightly from the others to remove a stone from her boot, and Lucinda took the opportunity to wait with her.

'Is everything okay, Lucinda? I mean, *really* okay?' Diana asked, sensing Lucinda wanted to get something off her chest.

Lucinda just smiled at Diana, before saying, 'Do you know what, I think so. I've got a plan.'

'That sounds dangerous,' Diana replied with a wry smile, before continuing, 'but be careful what you wish for. Things aren't perfect with Anthony, I know, but the grass isn't always greener on the other side. And sometimes you only really appreciate how good something is once it's gone.' Lucinda understood clearly the point she was making but also knew that her words weren't going to be enough to talk her out of it.

With that, Lucinda and Diana caught up with the rest of the group and continued on their way back to the house, ostensibly to prepare the tea. By the time the men had returned to the house, the women were finishing off their second bottle of Champagne as they shared stories by the fire in the sitting room.

A couple of the husbands came in and ran their cold, wet hands up the backs of their wives, leading to pleads of mercy from the women concerned and an eruption of laughter from the others. Needless to say, Anthony was not one of these men but instead watched on from the doorway with a forced smile, before announcing to himself only that he was going to skip tea and head up for a bath, if no one minded. Lucinda quietly slipped away from the group shortly afterwards and followed Anthony to their room, by which point he was already in the bath humming away as he always did.

Lucinda rested her head against the bathroom door and listened for a few moments. Perhaps now was the time to speak to him, rather than waiting until after Christmas. The weight she felt building up on her shoulders was becoming unbearable, and she wanted to get her announcement off her chest. She took a deep breath and opened the bathroom door.

'Hello, darling; I didn't hear you there at all,' Anthony said, sitting up in the bath. Lucinda looked on at him, with a growing sense of pity.

'Everything okay?' Anthony asked.

'Oh. Um, yes. Yes, all absolutely fine. I just wanted to check you had had a good day. That's all.'

'Very good, actually. Thanks, darling. Really enjoyed myself.'

'Great. Well, see you downstairs shortly.'

Lucinda closed the door and wondered to herself what she was thinking. Of course, now was not the right time to speak to him. No, she would stick to the original plan and wait until after Christmas. If that meant she had to carry the burden until then, then fine.

- Chapter Four -

Tulum, Mexico

The Christmas season in Tulum was the town's busiest period of the year, mostly for a mix of wealthy East Coast Americans and Europeans escaping away for some winter sun.

For Jack, however, his three-month stay in the beach town was approaching its end. Leonardo had already lined up another young traveller to take over Jack's position when he left. He was a 21-year-old man called Gabriel who lived an hour north of Los Angeles and had got in touch over Facebook six weeks ago. Leonardo had asked Gabriel to arrive a few days before Jack left so they could do a proper handover of responsibilities.

The downside of this was that Jack's already small yurt now had to accommodate two people, but the plus side was that he was now largely free to fully enjoy what remained of his time in Tulum without having to worry about the camp.

A week of partying culminated in Jack's final night at the Papaya Playa beach club, where they were hosting their legendary Christmas party, this year with Diego DJing.

Leonardo had already scheduled a "meditative healing group" on the beach at sunset, after which he and Jack planned to step it up a gear or three and head on to the party together.

To be truthful, Jack was yet to buy into the hype of beachside meditative healing in the way that so many other young people in Tulum did, but he didn't mind joining in occasionally.

Even though Leonardo swore by the homeopathic power of the "massage", Jack rather suspected it was, at least in part, the power of the unsuspecting female holiday-makers that led to his self-appointment as the local spiritual guru.

Jack had vaguely agreed to join Leonardo in this evening's session, and as he arrived at the scene, he immediately cursed himself for not having followed his own newly learnt but invaluable rule of extracting a specific job description out of his hippy friend. Leonardo had "forgotten" to mention the exact nature of today's class, which became clear to Jack only on reading the scrawled writing on the amateurish chalkboard outside the tent: *Tantric Meditative Healing*. Suffice to say, it didn't look like a normal yoga class.

Leonardo had only recently declared himself to be a tantric yoga instructor, having spent a weekend away with a supposedly qualified trainer he had met in a bar at the far end of the beach. She had taken him to a jungle retreat, two hours south of Tulum, where she had promised to train him up. What "training" actually took place during this time remained highly suspect, given the stories that Leonardo occasionally recounted.

Tonight's class was all about focussing upon the spiritual *yoni* massage – *yoni* being the Sanskrit name for a vagina – and it was a genre of class that Jack had thus far managed to avoid. At these evenings, often unlikely couples would sit facing each other, while Leonardo would demonstrate with his own partner, who was invariably the hottest attendee of the evening, how to release female sexual repression by opening up the energy channels inside her.

Increasingly, though, Leonardo had noticed that fewer couples were coming to the class and instead he had found a front row of single women, who were disconcertingly eager to offer their services for the demonstration, and partner with himself. That certainly changed the dynamic of the class, though on reflection he thought to himself that there could certainly be worse jobs.

On this particular evening, there were three different couples in the class, each looking around slightly awkwardly as they always did at the start.

To help them feel more at ease, Leonardo had set up a series of candles in glass lanterns in a circle, while a small Bose speaker played the requisite chanting music. Tonight was *Buddha Bar Chill*, Leonardo's go-to soundtrack.

Jack's job was to check off the names of the pre-booked list of guests who had paid $50 each for the hour's session.

Once Jack was happy that the whole class was present and correct, he nodded to Leonardo, who kicked off proceedings: 'Everyone, relax, and take long, deep breaths. Listen to the sound of the ocean and feel the energy of the earth beneath us. Move closer to your partner and feel the rhythm of your breathing together.'

Jack had just perched himself against a nearby sand dune, where he planned to contemplate the next chapter of his life until the class was over.

He had just started rolling himself a cigarette, when he spotted a couple of late arrivals: two middle-aged women, giggling nervously to each other. Jack jumped up to greet them.

The first woman seemed to be the instigator of their attendance. With thick, curly dark hair that fell just above her shoulders, she had a muscular physique and a large tattoo of a dragon down her right thigh.

The second woman was smaller, with mousey hair cut into a short bob, a nose piercing, and was wearing a green vest that hung loosely off her, exposing much of her chest as she leant forward. Both women were attractive in their own way, but years of sun and hard living were starting to creep into their faces. If he had to guess, Jack would say they were both about sixty but maintained figures that disguised their age.

'Can I help you ladies?'

'Yes, hi' said the first woman. 'I'm Chrissie and this is Noelle. We're here for the yoga class. We tried to book through our hotel, but they said it was too late and we were better off just turning up now to see if there's space.'

'Well, the class has literally just started, but I think it should be fine to join. Why don't you get started, and we can sort out the details later. If you'd both like to sit down opposite each other next to that couple in the corner, we can get started.' Jack pointed to a space, just at the back of the circle where the couples were now deep into the initial meditation stage.

The women paused and looked at each other before Chrissie blushed. 'Oh, thanks. But we're not here to massage each other! Not exactly lesbians.' She winked at her friend. 'We heard maybe there was an option to join the instructors?'

'Oh right. Um, okay. Hold on one sec; let me just check with Leonardo. He's the instructor.' Jack walked quietly to the front of the circle and whispered to his friend that he had two women who wanted to work with him as the instructor's demonstrator. Leonardo responded that he could only take one, and if they both wanted to join the class, Jack would have to partner with one of the women himself.

This was not something that Jack had ever thought he had signed himself up for, particularly given that it involved "partnering" with a woman the same age as his mother. But he was leaving Tulum in the morning and he had, after all, said to himself that he would throw himself into everything.

He looked back across the circle to Chrissie and Noelle. Chrissie, who already seemed to have started her own breathing exercises, was pumping herself up as if she was heading out into a boxing match. He frankly found her a little too intimidating and suspected she possessed an appetite for *yoni* stimulation beyond what he was experienced enough to provide.

Noelle, on the other hand, seemed rather less scary; perhaps even quite sweet. Through her wet, slightly sandy sarong, he could make out the pertness of her small bottom and felt he would be more than comfortable partnering up with her. He tapped Leonardo on the shoulder to confirm it was on and went back to the women to report the good news.

'Okay, Chrissie, if you want to go to the front and sit opposite Leonardo, you'll partner with him. Noelle, if you're comfortable with it, you and I will sit here together.'

'Great stuff, let's do this,' Chrissie replied, and made her way past the other couples to sit down opposite Leonardo.

'Okay, thanks,' Noelle said with just a fraction of a suppressed smirk apparent from the side of her mouth. She sat down next to Jack and crossed her legs tightly, doing her best to eliminate any feelings of nervousness.

After a couple more minutes of rhythmic breathing, Leonardo turned the music down slightly and began the main part of the class:

'My trusted friends, welcome to our sacred circle. Our intention today is to achieve three things: firstly, to heal any blocked sexuality inside us; secondly, to awaken our senses; and thirdly, to transform our minds. For us to succeed, it's important that we communicate clearly to our partners the boundaries and sensations with which we are comfortable.

'Now, I want everyone to stand up slowly and face your partner. Look deep into your partner's eyes, and sharing each other's energy, let us start to undress.'

At this point, Leonardo began walking slowly around the circle, talking to each of the couples in the group, reassuring the more apprehensive participants to release themselves into the circle of trust. He continued:

'As we remove each item of clothing, I want you to say out loud something in your lives that you have been harbouring and would like to release.'

'Sexual boundaries!' one woman shouted first as she removed her dress over her head.

'Judgement of others,' exclaimed one of the men.

'Preconceptions about age,' Noelle suddenly whispered to Jack, before dropping her sarong and untying the bows each side of her bikini bottoms, allowing them to drop to the floor. Her pubic area had been waxed nearly in its entirety, leaving just a thin strip of hair she'd left at the top of her crack. No doubt a special holiday haircut, Jack thought, as he noticed a small tattoo of a shooting star around an inch to the left of her clitoris.

Jack felt an unwelcome rush of blood in his body, pumping down towards his cock. He didn't know much about yoga, though he sensed getting a rock-hard erection was probably against the spirit of the class, and therefore did everything he could to block his mind from the vicinity of the shooting star sat opposite him.

He turned his thoughts as best he could to the lack of spice in his salsa plate he'd had for lunch, though despite his best efforts, his mind came racing back continuously to the naked woman in front of him, now staring intently into his eyes.

'Well done, everyone! Now, let's sit back in our cross-legged positions and breathe deeply again. Once you are fully relaxed, I want the women to wrap their legs around their partner, bringing your hips closer to each other. Once you're comfortable in that position, I want you to relax again and focus on your breathing.'

Jesus, Leonardo. What the hell have you got me into now? Jack fumed at Leonardo in his head, as Noelle wrapped her soft legs around him.

Unlike some of the other women in the group, Jack was pleasantly surprised by the obvious care and attention Noelle took in keeping her body hair well trimmed. She had the petite body of a woman considerably younger than her sixty years.

'When you're comfortable with your positions, I want the men to ask their partner's permission to enter their *yoni.*'

Noelle nodded, and Jack gently moved his index and middle fingers inside Noelle's vagina. On the instruction of Leonardo, he worked his fingers inside her, feeling for any tension built up within her, and applied pressure to her left side, then her right side and then up to the top. His fingers rotated gently in that order again, slowly massaging the inside of her increasingly wet vaginal lips.

'Now breathe deeply, and exhaaaale. Breath and exhaaaale, letting any tension out of you along with the air. We are in the sacred circle of trust here; release accordingly.'

41

At that point, moans of delight began to erupt around the circle of trust, with none louder than Chrissie who started rocking back and forth on her hips vigorously with what looked like most of Leonardo's hand now deep inside her.

Jack was trying to focus on Noelle only, but couldn't resist glancing at the other couples around the room. He was just thinking what a peculiar form of yoga this was that Leonardo had invented, when Noelle let out a cry and fell back onto the sand behind her, as if someone had taken a Taser to her body.

Soon, all the couples were lying on their backs, eyes closed, listening to the music Leonardo had turned back up.

'Feel the energy come up through your body, revitalising your *chakras*, connecting to your heart. Connecting to your soul. Allow that energy to float through you to your extremities and release it now through your hands and feet. Keep taking deep breaths and slowly come back up to a sitting position to face your partner. Put your hands together and thank your partner. *Namaste.*'

Once the last couple had left, walking back to their respective hotels hand in hand, Jack and Leonardo blew out the candles and packed up the rest of the equipment.

'Mate, I'm just going to put it out there. That was pretty weird. I didn't expect to spend my last night in Tulum sat in a candlelit circle full of naked people with my hand inside a woman the same age as my mother,' Jack said as he picked up the last of the mats.

'Fair enough, dude. I can't say I was expecting that either, but $600 for an hour's work isn't too bad at all.

And they all seemed to enjoy themselves, didn't they!'
Leonardo chuckled. 'C'mon, let's go get changed and head
to the beach party.'

*

Papaya Playa Beach Club was the area's original beachfront
party, with many of the best DJs in the world having played
there at some time or other. If you were in Tulum on a
Saturday night and you wanted a big party, then this was
the place to be found.

Although the music officially started around 10pm,
the club only got really busy at about midnight once the
restaurants in town had closed and all the European and
American seasonaires working there would then come
down to the party. Diego had the prime DJ set which was
due to start around 1am, and would finish up at sunrise at
around 6am.

Jack and Leonardo swung by one of the little bars on
the main strip of the town for some tapas and a couple of
drinks before arriving at Papaya Playa just after midnight.
As Saturday was the main changeover day, a lot of the guests
had just arrived that afternoon, and rather than succumb
to jetlag and tiredness, they were often raring to go.

There were three podiums built amongst the palm
trees, where a fire-dancing performance was in full swing,
with three women in leather Catwoman outfits dancing
while blowing fire towards the crowd.

Above the middle of the raving rabble floated a large
helium-filled skull, attached to the sandy makeshift dance

floor by a rope, in tribute to Mexico's tradition for the Day of the Dead.

Most of the women there were still wearing their bikini tops, some with t-shirts layered on top and which were invariably tucked into a tight pair of shorts. The men, like in much of Tulum, were a mix of buffed American finance guys in Ralph Lauren polo shirts which were slightly too tight and styled with the collar standing up, and Europeans wearing brightly coloured linen shirts who Jack felt looked altogether less intimidating. What they all had in common was an appetite to party.

Leonardo tried not to come to too many of these more commercial weekly parties, as he felt having twenty people dancing around his own campfire and listening to his own music was a far more authentic and natural experience than partying en masse. He was really there tonight to see Diego and give Jack a good send-off; contrary to his first impressions of a slightly stiff and uptight Brit, he'd enjoyed getting to know Jack far more than most of the guys who came through his camp.

He grabbed a tray from the bar and returned with four tequila slammers and four bottles of Corona, before he and Jack pushed through the crowd towards the bamboo DJ booth.

At the front of the dance floor nearest the DJ booth, Leonardo spotted two extremely beautiful women, one blonde and one brunette, dancing away, seemingly oblivious to the crowd of onlookers glancing on admiringly.

Without hesitation, Leonardo headed towards them with the tray of tequila slammers he had just picked up over his shoulder. Jack couldn't make out where he was headed, but by now knew Leonardo well enough not to ask questions.

When they reached the girls, the brunette turned towards them. Jack realised immediately it was Makenna, who had slipped away without a trace, leaving him to assume that she had already left Tulum.

'We thought you looked thirsty,' Leonardo said, as smooth as ever, handing each of the girls a tequila slammer and a Corona to wash it down. Jack and Makenna went along with their friends' assumptions that they hadn't met before, and Jack noticed that, as cool as before, Makenna showed no embarrassment at all at seeing him again. Each of them licked the side of their hand, sprinkled some salt on top of it, and then threw the double shot of tequila down their throats. To take away the harsh taste of the tequila, they each then took a large slice of lemon and sucked down hard on it, wincing slightly at its acidity.

'You left in a hurry the other night,' Jack whispered to Makenna, out of earshot of their friends.

'I know… I'm sorry. I should have said something, but you looked quite comfortable on the sand, and I knew I had to get back to our hotel before it became obvious to the others who I was with.'

'I get it,' Jack said with a smile, 'but it's a nice surprise to see you again. I thought you were leaving a few days ago?'

'Yeah, we were meant to, but my friend Candice here and I decided to stay through the weekend. LA-bound tomorrow. What about you?'

'Last night in paradise for me too. London calling. And, actually, there's no one else I'd rather be spending my last night with, if I'm being honest. I'm so pleased to see you again.'

'Oh, is that right, Mr Englishman? You think a girl falls twice for your accent, do you?' Makenna responded flirtatiously, moving her face slightly closer towards Jack before taking a swig of her Corona.

'One can only hope, I suppose,' Jack responded, moving his head a little closer still, while maintaining enough self-discipline to avoid going in for a kiss too soon, particularly in front of the others.

They were distracted from their near embrace by a roar from the crowd around them. Diego had put on his headphones and started spinning the Technics electronic DJ set in front of him. The crowd started bouncing.

Tonight, even by Papaya Playa standards, was going to be big, as the first Saturday of the Christmas holidays always was. But now that Jack had found Makenna, he felt he would rather be anywhere else with her at that moment, rather than in the sweaty pit of bodies on their first night in Tulum, going too hard and too fast. His Tulum, with Leonardo, had not been like this over the last three months. But Diego had got the place energised, as they all knew he would. Everyone around him seemed to be another drug-fuelled, drunken holiday-maker giving it everything they had. The thought didn't stop Jack repeating the tequila shot process with the others a few moments later when Leonardo returned with a refilled tray of drinks.

The music got louder; the beats got faster. Diego always tried to blend in an Aztec edge to his music, incorporating well-known dance anthems with a Mexican Mayan twist. The crowd were loving it, and as more people filled the dance floor, others spilled out beyond it onto the beach.

Makenna was wearing a black one-piece jumpsuit, revealing the whole of her toned, tanned back. Jack took the opportunity to run his hand down it, and then continued further, before resting it gently on Makenna's right buttock.

She responded by throwing her hair back and beginning to move her hips closer to him. Out of the corner of his eye, he could see Leonardo running his hands through Candice's hair, and starting to kiss the side of her neck. The movement of their bodies was mirroring Diego's beats.

The first thing Jack noticed about Makenna when he saw her last time was the way she moved her body to the music in a way he had never seen a woman do before. It was so effortless, yet so captivating to watch. Here she was doing it again and pulling him with her. Jack had never been particularly confident on the dance floor, but Makenna was guiding his body in a way which made him almost believe that he himself knew how to move.

She slowly and sexily spun around to face Jack. She put her arms around his neck and tossed her head back again to the sky, in exactly the same way she had the other night when she was naked in the ocean under the stars. Jack took the opportunity to take a prolonged glance at the full curvaceous breasts he had revelled in the night before.

Hand in hand, Jack moved their clutch up from her waist, across her chest, and then carefully over to the back of her head. Every part of him wanted to kiss her, but he knew she was leading the dance and would wait until she leaned into him. He closed his eyes and envisaged the next few hours, overjoyed to get another taste of this enchanting Californian chick.

At that point, her hand rested on his cheek, and she pulled his face towards her. He moved his mouth towards her. But just before their lips touched, they were made to leap apart by an excruciating screech from a concerningly familiar voice right next to them.

'Oh my GOD, it's the vagina massagers…!' Chrissie, who had clearly been continuing to throw back the tequila since they'd last seen her on the beach, appeared with a group of five other women, who must also have been approaching sixty, including Noelle.

Leonardo's embrace with Candice had also been brought to a rapid halt.

'These are the guys! The ones we were talking about. My God, WHAT this man did to me,' she said pointing at Leonardo. 'I mean, really, he put his entire arm inside me and introduced me to God. Where have you been all my life, and how much more of you can I have before I leave next week! My friends ALL want a go. Look at the smile on Noelle's face still. That's her partner there! Do you offer group discount?'

Candice and Makenna shared a puzzled look towards each other, amusedly digesting what they were hearing. They both readjusted their clothes.

'We'll see you around,' said Candice, before quietly slipping away into the crowd.

That wasn't how Jack had hoped the evening would pan out. The girl of his dreams had been right there, just a few moments ago, dancing with him. They were about to kiss, for God's sake. And now, he felt another hand rubbing his back. The hand of Noelle. Any thought of getting annoyed was short-lived, though, and he could only laugh to himself at the absurdity of the situation.

Fuck it, he thought to himself. It was nearly 2am, and his carnal instinct had kicked in. Makenna had disappeared into the crowd, and he knew there was no chance at this time of night of explaining what had just happened. While the thought of spending the rest of the night with Noelle wasn't quite how he had envisaged his last night being spent, the likely alternative at this point was spending it getting annihilated with Leonardo. Besides, Noelle had a good sense of humour and a surprisingly athletic body. Sleeping with women nearly forty years his senior wasn't something he was planning on making a habit of, but he saw no harm in indulging a bit more this one time.

He took Noelle's hand, who seemed slightly surprised at first. He smiled and gestured with his head for them to move away from the crowd and the over-excited hollering coming from Chrissie, who by now was literally bear-hugging Leonardo so tightly, it was unlikely he would be going anywhere soon. Noelle caught the eye of one of her other friends. The friend nodded, seemingly encouraging her to go with Jack. Given her friends now knew where

49

she was, she shrugged and allowed Jack to lead her away from the group through the crowd.

They were soon on the beach, behind the main dance floor, and began walking away from the party, shoes in hand and allowing the waves to wash over their feet. Once they were sufficiently far away to be out of sight, Jack led Noelle up from the beach and into the dunes.

Without a word, Noelle lay down on her back, and Jack lay next to her and began kissing her neck. Jack began whispering some irrelevant small talk to her, to which Noelle, in an uncharacteristic, dominant manner answered, 'No more talking, sportboy. I want you inside me.' Jack wasn't quite sure where the term "sportboy" had come from, but he got the gist of what she meant pretty clearly.

*

On realising Noelle and Jack had disappeared towards the beach, Chrissie decided to tighten her clutch on an increasingly uncomfortable Leonardo, going in for the lunge. Leonardo managed to turn slightly at the last minute to avoid his entire face being engulfed, before wriggling out of her sweaty clasp. Unlike Jack, Leonardo was not flying home in the morning and he had no intention whatsoever of taking things further with Chrissie.

Once he had escaped, he made an excuse and headed towards the relative safety of the VIP bar behind the DJ booth, where he stayed for the rest of the evening.

One of the increasingly popular traditions of the Papaya night was the random distribution of prizes and competitions. Mostly these were sponsored t-shirts or beachwear that a local brand would supply for some extra exposure. Occasionally, though, hotels liked to give away free accommodation as a branding opportunity on the particularly busy evenings.

Leonardo had agreed in a generous moment earlier in the season that he would contribute an entire week's free stay at Camp Mayo, and it happened that it was going to be given out that night. He thought he'd hang around then until the prize was awarded, before calling it a night.

At around 3am, it was announced they were going to give away the prize. The party organisers liked to give away the best prizes last to ensure people stayed late and spent as much money as possible in the process.

As with the previous prize-givings that had taken place, it followed the format of José, the lighting guy, focussing the spotlight beam from the top of the stage. It would move randomly over the crowd, before randomly landing on one of the guests when the music stopped.

Leonardo looked on across the crowd at the different faces, all jumping towards the travelling spotlight which continued to flick around the dance floor, before stopping just by the edge closest to the beach.

Leonardo looked towards the light of the spotlight just as Jack, who was leading Noelle by the hand back to the dance floor, inadvertently walked straight into it. They both froze upon realising that everyone was staring straight at them. Leonardo couldn't contain his laughter at the evident embarrassment on Jack's face, while secretly already hoping that this might mean his pal, given he had won, would come and visit him again soon. The waitress handed Jack his prize voucher before the spotlight was directed back to Diego and the stage.

Jack opened the envelope and read the card:

This voucher gives you a week's holiday at Club Mayo, Tulum. It includes all your drinks and food taken at Club Mayo, as well as a return economy class transport from a country of your choice courtesy of Iberia Airlines. Valid for six months only.

He and Noelle looked at each other awkwardly, before Jack handed her the envelope saying, 'You take this, Noelle. It's way easier for you to hop on a plane here than me.' He refrained from pointing out that, while he was just about to start work, Noelle had now all but retired and had a fair amount of spare time on her hands.

Noelle took the card gratefully and gave Jack a hug. 'You look after yourself, young man.' She kissed him one more time on the lips and turned to find her friends.

Assuming Leonardo would have already headed back to Camp Mayo, Jack headed towards the exit. He realised his car was coming in three hours, and he still needed to pack. At least he'd sleep on the flight! Unbeknown to him, though, Leonardo had seen the whole exchange since Jack had arrived back on the dance floor from his rendezvous on the beach.

He grabbed his shoulder. 'You, Jack Morley, are a mad English bastard, but I've loved getting to know you. I saw that whole scene unfold,' Leonardo said knowingly.

'You were watching us? Dude,' Jack responded.

'No! Fuck, God no! Not whatever the fuck you were doing to Noelle on the beach. I meant just now with the spotlight and the envelope and giving away the prize!'

Jack's face exposed a little relief, and Leonardo continued, 'Here, this was meant to be the prize for next month, but I want you to have this,' he said, before handing him a second envelope. 'Now you've got no reason not to come and visit me again!' It was a separate week's stay at Camp Mayo.

They hugged each other one last time before Leonardo headed back to the stage.

- Chapter Five -

Ferryman's Cottage, Norfolk

When Lucinda thought about the times she had been happiest since David had died, it had always been at Ferryman's Cottage during Christmas time.

From eccentric midnight mass services with the tipsy elderly vicar and children rushing down the stairs to find their stockings in the morning, to long, frosty Christmas morning walks before settling down around the fire to watch the Queen's speech, the whole family enjoyed Christmas.

Even this year, despite knowing it was going to be the last of its kind, Lucinda was looking forward to it. She hadn't seen much of Sophie and Jack in the last few months, what with Sophie now living up in Scotland and Jack being away travelling.

Sophie had studied History of Art at Edinburgh University and met Harry, her boyfriend, halfway through her second year. Harry's family ran a small, at least by Scottish standards, mixed estate up in the Angus Glens. Harry was a couple of years older than Sophie, and after graduating had spent two years working in Edinburgh as an analyst at a large pension fund company while Sophie finished her degree. He knew he was always going to have to return home to run the farm, perhaps sooner rather than later as his dad wasn't as young and healthy as he had once been, but he wanted to have at least some time working in the city before disappearing into the Scottish countryside.

They had met at a mutual friend's dinner party in a Georgian flat with high ceilings, which seemed much too grand for student digs, just off Dublin Street. Before that, he'd assumed he would head to London after university, like so many of his friends had done, but meeting Sophie had changed his mind. Perhaps if she had wanted to move down to the Big Smoke after graduating, he might have asked for a transfer to the London office, but at that point he was very happy to stay put.

Sophie graduated with a 2:1 and a tight group of university friends, and their relationship was still going well. With Harry having received a promotion to an associate, and no burning desire on the part of Sophie to leave Scotland, they decided it probably made more sense to stay in Edinburgh. It wasn't long before Sophie found a job at Lyon and Turnbull, the auction house headquartered in the Scottish capital.

They loved their time transitioning from students to young professionals in Edinburgh, and the lifestyle it gave them. Their flat, which they rented from a distant cousin of Harry's mother for a quarter of the market rate, had large neo-classical proportions and a lovely view out over the private gardens of Drummond Place, with the Firth of Forth just visible in the distance. It also had the added benefit of them both being able to walk to work – a far cry from the complaints of their London friends battling each morning on the underground.

After another two years, though, Harry's father found that his age was starting to catch up with him, and he knew his time to return home was approaching.

Sophie and Harry had discussed the move at length, and had agreed that when the time was right, they would throw themselves into it whole-heartedly, without looking back. So, when one January evening they were having a drink together in a wine bar off Queen Street, Harry nervously announced, 'I think it might be time to go home,' Sophie agreed immediately. Without drawing out the process, they both resigned from their respective jobs the following morning, and a month later they were in removal vans driving up the A90 past Dundee, and heading home.

It had long been assumed by Lucinda, Jack and Anthony that Sophie would marry Harry, but they couldn't predict when. They had enjoyed visiting the young couple in Edinburgh, which was lucky, given Sophie's reluctance to leave the city. The flight from Norwich to Edinburgh was hugely convenient for short trips up to Scotland, and they made the journey fairly regularly, often staying at The Scotsman Hotel just on the Old Town side of the George IV Bridge.

Lucinda was fond of Harry, and any regret she had at not seeing more of her daughter was outweighed by the comfort of knowing Sophie had found a man she clearly adored and who, evidently, reciprocated her feelings. In some ways, there were elements of David, Sophie's father, about him in his gregarious, enterprising outlook on life.

Jack, who had studied Geography at Newcastle University, enjoyed having his sister just up the road for the two years that their university days overlapped, and visited her regularly. This usually entailed camping on Sophie's sofa in Edinburgh, but he also made a few trips up to Glen Clova with his sister, Harry and a gaggle of friends.

On a good run, you could get to Harry's farm in two hours from Edinburgh, and once there they had the glen right on their doorstep, offering about as much fun as young students could have. Long summer days led to swimming in the nearby loch or stalking deer off the hill, but they were mostly there in the winter when they bunkered down by fires after causing mischief in the snow.

Lucinda did sometimes wonder whether she would have had the same firm inclination to leave Anthony had her children not been away *quite* so much. Or perhaps she should have been busier on her own projects; she used to spend days working on her watercolours in the summerhouse, and why didn't she take on one of Diana's adorable Labrador pups last year?

Doubt crept into her previously clear mind. Was she partly to blame after all? She mulled the idea as she unloaded the Waitrose carrier bags from her car, before quickly assuring herself that her situation was in fact entirely down to Anthony's dreariness, and had very little, if anything, to do with her own shortcomings.

That's enough of those thoughts, she told herself, and focussed her attention back on to Jack's return that evening. Sophie would also start the drive down from Angus that day, but planned to break up the journey by spending the night with friends near Ripon in Yorkshire en route, before arriving home in time for lunch tomorrow. Harry, dedicated as ever, would be staying on the farm in Scotland, as the livestock needed tending to.

*

Lucinda arrived at Downham Market station ten minutes before Jack's train was due to pull in. This gave her enough time to grab a coffee from the recently opened café on the platform, aptly named The Platform, which had until recently been a public lavatory.

The local MP, Tricia Wilson (or Dishy Trishy, as most of the men in Norfolk referred to her), had proudly opened it the week before to a small public audience and the local newspaper, the *Eastern Daily Press*.

It was all part of a local government drive to bring more jobs to East Anglia in an attempt to diversify the economy away from agriculture. MPs with rural constituencies, such as West Norfolk, had been warned centrally by the Department for Environment, Food & Rural Affairs that their efforts to reduce intensive farming in the UK would have a likely short-term negative impact on the local jobs market. Therefore, anything that could be done to help create small businesses in the region would be prioritised. As a result, the new owners of The Platform had almost been given the premises for free by the local council in order to get it going, and Dishy Trishy was ensuring she milked every bit of credit for its opening.

Lucinda found herself thinking it was going to take an awful lot more than The Platform coffee shop to offset the reduction in local farming shops, but it was a surprisingly good cappuccino.

She spotted Jack's face in the window of the penultimate carriage before the train had pulled in, or perhaps it was his blue North Face backpack that she recognised first.

The scrum of commuters and children, most of whom were also rushing home to friends and family for the Christmas holidays, swept past her as she waited for Jack to get his bags together.

Lucinda hugged him ever so slightly harder than she would have done in previous years, knowing that this familiar annual routine might not happen again in the same way. Jack's hair had grown and he looked like he needed a good wash, but otherwise she was pleased to see he had returned from his travels seemingly unscathed. No tattoos and no pregnant Mexican girlfriend – *can't wish for more than that*, she told herself.

Back at Ferryman's Cottage, Anthony had got the fire going for their return, and as they came through the door, Jack hugged his stepfather with genuine affection.

Lucinda felt Anthony had many shortcomings, but she could not fault the way he had supported her with Sophie and Jack. From taking them to school sports clubs every weekend, to driving them back from parties late at night throughout their teenage years, he had been nothing but devoted to the children.

That night, after the three of them had had supper and gone to bed, Lucinda lay awake as Anthony snored gently with his back to her. Uneasily, she thought again to herself about how much she would miss Christmas at Ferryman's, the four of them together.

But her mind quickly and excitedly drifted on to what life would be like in January. Would she ask Anthony to leave, or would she leave herself – and if she went, then where would she go? And who actually owned the house now? She hadn't thought about that. She had far more friends nearby than Anthony, but she knew that wouldn't really bother him if he insisted on staying. He hardly saw anyone as it was, and she suspected that the upheaval of having to move somewhere else would concern him more. Besides, she liked the thought of spending some time away. As it was to be an adventure, perhaps somewhere warm.

She had a cousin, Pauline de Westholz, who ran a vineyard in South Africa, about an hour outside Cape Town in the Franschhoek Valley. She had been promising to visit her for years, so perhaps now was the time. She could even help them run the wine-tasting room, or even cook in the new vineyard bistro that they wrote about in this year's Christmas round robin.

Lucinda was a recent convert to Instagram and was always seeing pictures that Pauline and her South African husband, Greg, were posting about how busy they were with visitors. It had mainly been just English visitors for a long time, but for the last couple of years there had been frequent coachloads of Chinese tourists arriving. Although it made the farm seem a little more commercial, Greg happily pointed out to his wife that while the English rarely bought much more than a token bottle after a wine tasting, the Chinese guests regularly left with a case of his most expensive signature blend. He'd even increased the price of the Pinotage three times now to keep up with demand.

Yes, a few months in the Cape sounded like a good plan, and the very idea made her relax. She rolled over and closed her eyes. Tomorrow was Christmas Eve, and Sophie would be home.

Christmas Eve at Ferryman's Cottage had followed the same jolly routine for as long as they had been there. After the four of them had supper, they settled in front of the fire to play a game of animal charades. Loosened by the three bottles of claret from Anthony's collection, in addition to the two bottles of Champagne they had already drunk before supper, they were all suitably amused by the time they left the house and crossed the village green to get to the beautiful medieval church of St James's for their annual midnight mass service.

Compared to the rest of the congregation, though, they seemed relatively sober. The Turners, who lived in the large rectory on the other side of the village and generally had a party of fourteen or so with various cousins staying, could be counted on for being the most raucous. That was, of course, not including Reverend Peter, who had retired fifteen years ago but agreed to continue to do the service. His life mostly revolved now around his fabulous collection of single malts and his Norwich Terrier, Monty, who accompanied him to the service and even enthusiastically joined in some of the hymns, somewhat bolstering the warbling from the much-admired geriatric "choir".

Despite the service finishing after midnight, each year the congregation would stay for a glass of celebratory Champagne with Reverend Peter, fearing it might be his last. It never was, and each Christmas morning, most of Castle Acre would wake up even more hungover than they would have been anyway.

This Christmas turned out to follow the usual agenda precisely, and the four of them appeared downstairs for breakfast just after 9am, with heads far rougher than any of them would care to admit.

Sophie helped Lucinda prepare the turkey that had been delivered the day before by a nearby farmer friend, while Anthony and Jack cleared up the final bits of mess from the night before and started re-laying the table ahead of the late lunch. Once the turkey was in the oven, and the table was beautifully laid, they wrapped up in their coats and headed out for a stomp.

The River Nar was just at the bottom of their lane, and their walking route had barely changed since they moved to Castle Acre. From the house, they headed straight past the church and then to the ruins of a monastic priory, dating back to 1090. From there, they would reach the

River Nar and follow the river downstream until it took them into the ancient woods ahead. The huge branches of the oak trees above cast shadows against the meandering banks of the river. Robins, goldfinches and, on occasion, blue tits, would dart around overhead seeking food morsels dropped on the path by walkers emptying their pockets.

On entering the woods, the ancient oak trees appeared still and silent around them, yet after focussing further it became clear that there was, in fact, a buzz of activity from wildlife and nature everywhere you looked. Lucinda had taken this walk thousands of times since she moved to Ferryman's Cottage, but each time something was different. That's what drew her back, time and time again.

You knew you'd come to the end of the woods once you could see the four-storey mill appearing between the opening in the trees. The Mill House dated back to the late 18th century, and had fallen into disrepair until it was bought a few years ago by a surgeon from London.

The surgeon had totally refurbished it with love, taste and not an insignificant sum of money, and it stood proudly once more over the banks of the River Nar. On the other side of the house was a ford, where children would play Poohsticks and dogs would swim before inevitably vigorously shaking dry their fur by an innocent passer-by. Often one activity would interrupt the other, meaning that clear Poohstick victories were becoming increasingly rare, but they all worked it out in the end.

At the ford you would cross the river and come back on yourself on the other side by climbing the banks of the valley where the flowing water had cut into the hill, leaving a landscape resembling cascading waterfalls of soil, mud and rabbit holes.

From the top of the valley you could look down on Castle Acre village in its full glory. It stretched from the ruined priory and the church onto the Ostrich pub in the centre of the handsome village, before reaching the Old Bailey Gate and, finally, the remains of the castle itself, which had been an old Norman fort.

There they sat, looking down on the village, towards Ferryman's Cottage. Smoke still faintly billowed from the chimney where Anthony had restarted the fire after breakfast, before triple-checking that he had put the fireguard in place as they left the house.

'Merry Christmas, guys,' said Sophie, breaking the silence. 'Much as I love this spot, it's getting seriously cold and, aren't some elves due back in the kitchen?'

Sophie linked arms with Jack and pulled him back down the hill towards the river crossing at the bottom. Unlike the previous ford near the Mill House, which was well signposted, this one was more of a car undercarriage booby trap, and entirely unsuitable for normal vehicles to use. That didn't stop satnav continuing to send poor, unsuspecting drivers through it, only to lose a significant part of their car in the process and sometimes even require rescuing.

*

Back at the house, Anthony bellowed life back into the embers of the fire before throwing on some extra logs, while Lucinda and Sophie perched themselves on the sofa next to the pile of presents surrounding the foot of the Christmas tree. They had an hour until the Queen's speech was broadcast, after which they would sit down for lunch.

Jack had bought Sophie a beautiful aquamarine necklace from a trinket seller in Tulum. Blown away by his own generosity with her gift, he realised somehow, incomprehensibly, he'd forgotten to get a present either for his mother or Anthony.

Shit, he thought to himself, *all this time I've had. Even yesterday in London, and I completely forgot to get them anything. Anything at all.*

'C'mon, Jack, we're just waiting for you now,' shouted Sophie from the sitting room.

'Will be right there, give me one sec. Just need to... finish something...' Jack shouted back.

'It's a bit late now for Christmas shopping, Jack!' Sophie responded, semi-jokingly.

Anthony got up from his armchair by the fireplace and went to the kitchen. He returned shortly afterwards with four glasses and a fresh bottle of Champagne. 'Well, we might as well have a drink while we wait.'

Upstairs, Jack frantically emptied out his bag, hoping to find something he had picked up on his travels that could be wrapped up as a present, but short of a pair of Havana flip-flops or the new Ray-Ban sunglasses he'd bought duty free at the airport, it wasn't looking good.

He had seen something on a film last year about a boy giving his grandparents "time" as a present, meaning he wrote twenty-four hours on a piece of paper and allowed his grandfather to decide what to do with it.

Somewhat corny, perhaps but, given the current lack of alternative options, he might just have to give it a try.

He searched his room for a piece of paper, before grabbing one from the printer he had under the desk. In his backpack, he knew he had a pen and went rummaging through the endless scraps inside it as he reached for it. As he dug deeper, he came across an envelope which he was about to discard before he twigged. It was the holiday prize that Leonardo had so generously handed him at Papaya Playa.

Daft bloody Leonardo, he thought affectionately, wondering if his friend would ever wake up to the real world. Jack's new job was starting in the New Year, and he knew there would be no way he would be able to go back to Tulum within six months.

Then the idea occurred to him. He was in dire need of finding a present for his parents, who themselves had plenty of time on their hands. 'Genius,' he muttered, congratulating himself as he realised that giving the voucher to his mother and Anthony would kill two birds with one stone. The parents would be delighted – it would definitely be the most generous gift that year – and Leonardo's voucher wouldn't go to waste.

Sure, Tulum, especially not Club Mayo, perhaps wouldn't be their traditional choice of holiday, but there was lots to do there beyond the clubbing and dancing. TheAztec ruins, for example, and plenty of beaches and restaurants.

Besides, it would do them some good, Jack thought, to have a little adventure together. Although Jack was blissfully unaware of his mother's plan to leave Anthony in the New Year, even he could appreciate their life had become a little lacklustre recently. *In fact, it's literally exactly what they need right now*, his thought process continued. What's more, it was guaranteed to be better than whatever present Sophie had got them. So why not? The only thing that they didn't need to know was how or why he had ended up in possession of the envelope in the first place.

He delved into the hall cupboard, which contained a disorderly collection of random bits and pieces, including wrapping paper, and tried his best to make his parents' present look like it had been considered before 2pm on Christmas Day itself. Satisfied with his wrapping, which, after all, had never been a strong point, he drew a couple of smiley faces on the envelope and headed back downstairs.

'What've you been up to? I didn't know Amazon offered extra-special instantaneous delivery,' Sophie probed once more, with the bottle now almost empty.

'Must admit I did forget to wrap something, that's all. Right, who's first?'

Sophie began handing out the presents, and the four family members each took great interest in watching who had been given what by whom. First, there was a thick green wool cardigan that Lucinda had given Anthony; Sophie had got her mother some of her favourite Aromatherapy Associates bath oil; Lucinda gave Jack a large box of wine from Majestic and a new brown wax jacket; and Anthony handed Lucinda a small rectangular box with Monica Vinader printed on the side. Somewhat surprised, she opened it to find an 18ct gold chain with a diamond-encrusted pendant on the end.

She recognised it immediately. One of Diana's more fashionable friends, Sarah, had been wearing the same design during their weekend at Bickham Hall, fetching compliments from all of the female guests. Either Anthony had been paying more attention that weekend than she had realised, or more likely, Diana was involved in the selection of the gift, which was as much unexpectedly thoughtful as it was inconvenient, given Lucinda's intentions.

Regardless of the timing, she was quietly touched by Anthony's efforts. His response, of course, had been a gentle pat on her leg and a mumble of, 'So glad you like it, darling.'

'Gosh! I ought to hurry up and get the rest of lunch ready—' Lucinda announced as she looked at her watch, in an attempt to distract from having given Anthony a rather obviously less considered present.

'Well, hang on, Mum. Don't be so rude! I haven't even given you your present yet,' Jack interrupted, grinning. He continued, 'In fact, it's a joint present this year. To you and Anthony, and I think you'll both *really* like it.'

He handed them the envelope as Sophie looked on with intrigue from the corner of the room.

Lucinda opened the first layer of wrapping paper before handing the envelope to Anthony to open. He pulled out the card, perched his glasses on the end of his nose and started reading.

'A week's holiday in Club Mayo, Tulum.' Lucinda's faced dropped. 'Well, that sounds lovely, Jack. How generous! Thank you very much indeed. Now what on earth is Club Mayo, Tulum?'

'It's where he's just returned from, Anthony,' fumed Lucinda, with a little more aversion to the idea than Jack had anticipated. 'I mean, it's a *traveller's* destination. Of course we can't go, Jack! We're not on our gap year! What are you thinking?' Lucinda said.

'That's not actually true, Mum. It's just been voted CNN traveller destination of the year, with some of the best beaches, spas and restaurants in the world. And there's no better place on the coast to base yourself than Club Mayo,' Jack retorted, having memorised the branding on the back of the leaflets Leonardo gave him to hand out as one of his first jobs on arrival.

- Chapter Six -

Castle Acre, Norfolk

Boxing Day had been spent with the Turners, who had their annual family rough shoot, based around their relatively small area of woodland.

Norfolk was known for having many first-class shoots, but the Turners' was most certainly not one of them. It did, however, have the benefit of bordering a large commercial shoot on one side, so by positioning a number of bird feeders on the borders of their wood they were able to entice in a few of the thousands of pheasants and partridges that lived nearby in order to have their little family shoot once a year. The aim of reaching double digits was nearly always proven to be too ambitious, and the previous year they only managed one cock pheasant and two pigeons.

With all the Turner cousins and uncles staying, plus Jack and Anthony, they had twelve men shooting. Together they formed "the guns". Unlike proper shoots where a team of beaters would efficiently flush out birds using dogs to fly over the waiting guns, the Turners' shoot worked by splitting the twelve guns into two teams of six, which they split between the two generations. The logic was then that the teams would push the birds towards each other and shoot them as they came over.

Freddy Turner, the eldest of the brothers, would give the safety briefing beforehand, which always consisted of the same sentence: 'You've all done this before, and therefore you know that this is by far the most dangerous form of shooting there is. Make sure you see sky where you aim, particularly towards the end of the walk. And as you know, the team with the fewest kills at the end will receive the forfeit.'

The forfeit was always the same: a skinny dip into the River Nar after lunch, which the younger generation had (willingly) received for the last three years. Naturally, the senior crew put this down to skill, while the youngsters mumbled something about the positioning of the feeders as they raced down to the river wearing absolutely nothing, while trying to keep their footing in the deep, muddy puddles.

The first team, which was mainly the younger generation, including Jack, would march a mile down the lane to the far side of the wood and would walk in from the rear. Freddy Turner, the eldest of the brothers, was still considered the younger generation, as his father, Bill, now ninety-one, would insist on joining the shoot each Boxing Day. With the help of a 28-bore shotgun and an electric wheelchair, Bill would take his position on the lawn by the front of the house. He hadn't shot anything for years, and some doubted whether it was wise for him to even handle live ammunition, but everyone accepted that only death would stop him participating, preferably his own.

Meanwhile, the rest of the older generation team would line up on the front side of the house, facing the woods. At 10am precisely, both teams would start walking towards each other, apart from Bill, who would stay exactly where he was in case anything flew back over.

As they set off, an early pigeon flew up which Anthony picked off surprisingly well, given how rarely he shot these days. A roar went up from the older generation. This would happen every time a shot was fired, regardless of whether anything was actually hit or not, as a way of sledging their opponents into a false sense of concern.

A few moments later, two pheasants got up right in front of Martin Turner, Freddy's youngest brother, who raised his gun as quickly as he could but missed with both barrels. Anthony watched one of the pheasants turn towards the house, while the other one turned back towards him. He raised his gun and fired, bringing the cock pheasant down cleanly right on the feet of his neighbour. A roar went up again but was brought to a swift end by the sound of another shot from behind them. Everyone fell totally silent before they heard high-pitched shrieking from the direction of the house. Contrary to the whole team's initial fears, it wasn't because of a deathly misfire from Bill, but instead he had hit the stray pheasant which had then landed very nearly on his head, a sign of a good shot taken out in front.

'Surely old Bill's bird counts for double?' shouted someone on the line, reminding the team that it was the first bird he had shot in years from his position on the lawn.

'It might well do,' Robert, the middle Turner brother, responded, 'particularly if Martin continues to miss everything in sight!' jabbing at his brother's earlier miss. The older generation were already 3-0 up, which, if last year was anything to go by, would secure them victory.

For a brief moment, silence fell and all you could hear was the sound of twigs cracking under strides of Wellington boots as the teams marched forward, deeper into the wood. By the time both lines were within 20 yards of each other, several further shots and roars of delight had taken place, and knowing it was close, everyone grinned at their opposite man enthusiastically, waiting for the count. Just as Freddy lifted his arm and raised the whistle to his lips to signal the end of the shoot, bang! Another shot was fired.

They quickly realised that the shot must have been old Bill again in his chair, but unlike last time, there was no sound of a subsequent roar. Either he had missed, or the long-suffering women standing with him had had enough of the nonsense and gone back inside.

Both sides emptied their bag. Two partridges and a pheasant from the young, and two pheasants and a pigeon from the old. Everyone shook hands and turned back towards the house, carrying the game with them. It seemed the younger generation had escaped their skinny dip in the icy river this year.

Arriving back in high spirits, they found Bill in his electric chair, gun broken on the ground, pointing a stick towards a thick bramble bush behind a nearby yew tree.

He was using the stick to command his granddaughters, Tasha, Alice and Sophie, and Antonia, one of the grandchildren's girlfriends, to search for something in the brambles on their hands and knees.

Just as the guns were approaching behind him, Antonia jumped up with a yelp, holding a dead squirrel by its tail. Old Bill's squirrel had given the older generation the win for the fourth consecutive year, in the most triumphant of circumstances.

The younger generation handed their guns over and headed down to the river for their forfeit. As he entered the silty river, naked and shivering, for the fourth year in a row, Jack questioned why his Boxing Days always ended up like this. But as soon as he submerged his head under the frosty water, which despite evidence of global warming elsewhere in the world seemed to get colder every year, he knew in his heart that there was nowhere else he would rather be at that moment.

From the large bay windows of the Turners' Georgian rectory, Lucinda looked on at the river with the other women, all of whom were in hysterics at the scene of nudity unfolding below.

While the boys were swimming, Anthony and Robert had snuck down to the river and grabbed the clothes left by Jack and Freddy, who were now chasing them up the banks of the river, while desperately trying to preserve what little dignity they had left, having been fully submerged in freezing water just moments ago.

Lucinda wondered what on earth had got into Anthony. He never got this stuck in. Then there was the

Christmas necklace she had agreed to wear today, even though it was hidden underneath her thick, cashmere polo-neck jumper. Christ, he was even starting to look like a good shot!

As the whole episode unfolded, she hadn't noticed Diana arriving for lunch. She'd been carefully watching Lucinda's reaction and was pleased to see her smiling even if she did look a little surprised. Coming up from behind, she said quietly to Lucinda,

'You're not still thinking of doing anything silly, are you?'

Lucinda, somewhat caught off guard, composed herself before saying simply,

'Diana, how lovely to see you, and Happy Christmas.'

Though she had given nothing away, Diana looked at her knowingly, with one eyebrow sharply in the air.

Unbeknown to either of them, Sophie had been perching on the sofa behind them both, and observed their exchange curiously.

*

Back at Ferryman's Cottage later that afternoon, Sophie began packing up her bags, before making the long journey back up to Angus in the morning. Jack was staying another day, before heading to London to prepare for his job starting the following week, and to move his belongings into his new home for the year, renting a room off his friend Archie on the New King's Road.

While Jack ran a hot bath, he opened up the Iberia Airlines website to finalise the flight dates for Anthony and Lucinda's trip. He knew that if he didn't sort it out straight away, then it probably wouldn't happen at all.

He entered the voucher code he'd been given into the website, which opened up all available flight options. But just like his previous attempts to book trips on air miles, "all" of the options amounted to just three different dates over the next six months. The best he could find were flights from Heathrow via Madrid, and returning via Houston to Madrid, and then Madrid back to London. And they left in precisely one week's time.

Next to the booking option there was a little flag saying only two seats were remaining, so Jack, decisive as ever, felt that it would be too risky to waste time getting out of the bath, drying himself off, heading downstairs and checking with his mother and Anthony. Instead, he just booked the flights there and then.

Booking confirmed. Great! He carefully put the iPad down on the floor, wrapping the towel around the screen to stop any water splashing on it, and submerged himself in the bath, ensuring that any leftover dirt from the river was removed.

*

The following morning, they had a final breakfast together before Sophie took off back to Angus to see Harry.

'So, when are you guys heading to Mexico?' Sophie asked across the dining room table.

'I'm not sure. Jack, do you know how we get it booked?' Anthony asked, before Lucinda, who was looking down at the table, could say anything.

She had tried to forget about the Mexico trip, rather hoping if nothing was said, it could just be forgotten about.

Sensing that he might have acted with a little too much haste for his parents' leisurely pace of life, he replied sheepishly, 'Oh, um, actually yep, I thought I'd help you with that before I left. In fact, I already have. You leave from Heathrow at 10am next Monday,' Jack responded, trying to drop their departure date into the conversation nonchalantly.

'What? As in six days' time? Jack, are you *quite* mad? This is a ridiculous idea. I can't possibly do that. I haven't planned anything or even thought about my packing, not to mention what to do when we're there,' said Lucinda, evidently flustered.

Lucinda's reaction was expected by Jack and Anthony, but Sophie, who was secretly a little envious of the trip, seemed a little more surprised. Her mind sprung back to the conversation she had overheard her mother having with Diana the day before.

'Well, darling, I think I'll be fine by then. Just need some beach stuff and sunglasses, right?' Anthony cheerfully chipped in.

'Exactly, Anthony. That's all you need.' Jack responded, before adding: 'In fact, here's your flight itinerary,' handing over a printed piece of paper.

Lucinda felt ambushed. She didn't really know what to say. In her mind, Christmas had been exactly as she had hoped, and a fitting final chapter to what had been, in her eyes at least, a lonely and disappointing period of her life.

She looked at her children and then briefly across to Anthony, who was studying the flight itinerary with intrigue, in particular the three-legged journey in economy on the way home.

Lucinda took a deep breath and composed herself. What was one more week in the bigger picture? She could use the trip to talk things through with Anthony and could still be holding wine tastings in the Cape by mid-January, perhaps even with a base tan, she thought to herself.

'Great. Thank you, darling. You are a thoughtful boy,' Lucinda smiled, as he passed her the flight itinerary.

*

Jack carried Sophie's bags down the stairs for her, and out to her VW Golf parked outside.

'Jack, do you think everything's okay between those two?' she asked her brother.

'As okay as it's ever been, I'd say. I thought they were quite happy actually over the last few days. Didn't you?'

'I don't know. It's just something Diana said to her, as if she knew something was up. Oh, I dunno. Maybe I'm imagining it.'

'I think sometimes Mum thinks too much about this sort of stuff. She needs to chill out more generally, but I think they're fine and happy muddling on. Besides, it's not like they've got things too tough, is it? And that was sweet, the necklace that Anthony got her.'

'Yeah, you're probably right. Besides, maybe your mad Tulum idea will do them some good.'

'Let's see. Now drive carefully, and tell Harry I'll be up to see you guys soon.'

'You better had. And good luck with the new job. And life in London, for that matter. I dread to think what you and Archie are going to get up to in your bachelor pad.'

Jack laughed and lifted the rest of her bags into the car while Sophie went in to say goodbye to Anthony and Lucinda.

As Sophie got into her car, her phone rang. It was Harry. She silenced it, deciding that it would make more sense to call him back once she was out of the village and back on the A47 where she wouldn't have to concentrate so hard on the winding lanes. But he called again, and she answered.

It turned out that Harry just wanted to wish Lucinda and Anthony a quick Happy Christmas. Sophie moaned that he should have called earlier, before reluctantly getting back out of the car and passing the phone to Lucinda. They spoke briefly before she passed the phone to Anthony.

Anthony's conversation followed the normal niceties you would expect, before he walked slightly further down the lane in what looked like an effort to pick a sloe from the bush, despite knowing they had all been picked back in November.

'Anthony, do hurry up! Sophie must be on the road soon, or she'll never get home,' Lucinda barked before leading Sophie back inside to the warmth.

Unbeknown to the slightly cross women, Harry had asked Anthony to move out of earshot of the others, hence his appalling sloe-picking acting skills. Once Anthony confirmed he couldn't be overheard by the others, Harry's tone changed.

'Anthony, I know you're not Sophie's father, but you've been a terrific support for her entire life, and I know she loves you very much. I wanted to ask you if you would be prepared to allow me to marry her. I was planning on asking her tomorrow.'

'Ah, yes, Harry, very good of you, very good of you. Of course, I'm not Sophie's father, you're right. But if I were, I would not hesitate at all. I know Lucinda and I would be more than delighted if you two were to be married.'

'Is that your blessing then, Anthony?'

'Well, you would have it, of course, but I fear it would be presumptuous of me. It is only for Sophie to answer this.'

'You're a decent man, Anthony. I'll take that as I may. That's why Sophie's so fond of you. Thank you.'

Anthony put the phone down and walked back to the house.

'What on earth were you talking about out there for so long?' Lucinda asked.

'He, um, well, he wants to make us some sloe gin, you see. As a Christmas present. And, well, he just wanted to find out if one of the sloes he was using would be too far gone to be used still. It being December and everything.'

Lucinda and Sophie, who had now reappeared, looked on confused, but they were used to Anthony's incomprehensible waffle by now and they suspected that as so often happened, he probably totally misunderstood the conversation. After all, Harry, a farmer, who grew crops for a living, seeking Anthony's advice on bottling his sloe gin, did seem a little peculiar.

*

The following day, Jack jumped on the train back to London, swapping his backpack and hiking shoes for a suit bag, a number of shirts, many of which had belonged to his father, and a couple of suitcases.

Back at Ferryman's Cottage, Lucinda and Anthony were alone again.

'I enjoyed that Christmas, darling. Very much, in fact,' Anthony said, pouring himself a glass of claret from one of the few Christmas bottles that hadn't been drunk.

'Yes, it was a success, wasn't it?' said Lucinda, before changing the subject. 'Anthony? Look, do you *really* think we need to go to Mexico. Don't you think we'll find it all, well, hellish? With all that loud music, and young people dancing around the beach?'

'Well, actually, I looked it up online, and there does seem to be quite a lot to see there. And I thought we might even book a fishing trip; there are meant to be terrific marlin in that part of the world, you know.'

'No, Anthony, I didn't know...' Lucinda sighed, speaking to herself. How quiet the house suddenly felt again, without Sophie and Jack.

- Chapter Seven -

From Castle Acre, Norfolk to Tulum, Mexico

4 am is a wholly ungodly time for anyone to have to get up, Lucinda thought to herself as she lifted her suitcase into the back of their Volvo. But if they were to get to Heathrow on time, Anthony insisted that it was essential to leave by then in order to avoid the rush hour traffic and catch their flight.

Well, it was if you were Anthony, who liked to get anywhere, but especially airports, with plenty of time to spare. In the end, traffic wasn't as bad on the A1 as Anthony had envisaged and, as Lucinda had predicted, they arrived at Terminal 5 with a little over three and a half hours to spare.

'Perfect. We'll find a nice little cafe to have some breakfast and settle down with a newspaper,' Anthony reassured her, in an effort to squeeze some sort of smile out of her.

*

After a further eighteen hours of travelling, very little sleep and much discomfort, they landed in Cancun Airport at 9.30pm local time. Looking out of the window during the landing, all Lucinda could see was one concrete breeze block hotel after the next, and the neon lights of fast food parlours. She wanted to cry. She was tired, starving (having turned down Anthony's invitation to an airport breakfast out of principal and then refusing to eat any economy class food for the entire journey) and just wanted to be in her own bedroom back home again. Meanwhile, Anthony seemed to have watched a movie about Christopher Robin, which Lucinda was sure had been made for children, had three gin and tonics, and then slept the rest of the way.

Getting off the plane did little to change her mood. The humidity in the air, even at 9.30pm, brought her out in a hot flush. Once they'd retrieved their bags and made it through customs, they were relieved to see a sign with their name on it being held amongst the others, whereupon they followed their driver to a waiting white minibus. Having squeezed on, they found two other couples and a group of four young men sitting on the back row, each of whom seemed to look, dress and style their hair in exactly the same way as Jack on his arrival at Downham Market just before Christmas.

It took another ninety minutes to reach Tulum, and Lucinda spent much of this part of the journey mentally cursing her son for putting her through this. She was pleasantly relieved, though, to see that after just forty minutes of driving away from Cancun, the large concrete resorts petered out and were replaced instead with jungle and darkness.

They turned off the main 307 Highway running from Cancun along the coast, eventually hitting Belize, and the minibus made its first stop at an Argentinean hotel, a vast open structure built in the shape of a boat, and intricately decorated with woven twigs as the sail, and which even Lucinda admitted looked to be an architectural triumph.

The wave of optimism that Lucinda felt was short-lived, though, as one of the couples climbed out of the minibus and she was able to take a closer look. Even with a limited grasp of Spanish and in her tired state, Lucinda was pretty confident that "naturalista" meant it was a nudist hotel. She closed her eyes and cursed Jack again.

A few minutes later, the minibus stopped again, this time at what looked like a rather more civilised guesthouse, Lucinda thought. Hacienda San Angel, this one was called, designed in more of a traditional Aztec style, with an appealing and brightly coloured restaurant with it too. The other couple got out.

'Anthony, write down the name of that hotel, please,' she told Anthony, not caring that she was in earshot of the others on the bus.

'Whatever for, Lucinda? Jack's already sorted ours for us,' he queried.

'Precisely. If we find that it's ghastly, as I suspect it will be, I want to go and stay right there.' She pointed to the smiling receptionist helping the second couple, and who had just been offered refreshing-looking cocktails on a tray covered in fresh pink petals.

'Oh, darling,' he smiled, a little too patronisingly for her liking. 'Jack told me it was very comfortable. Why on earth would it be ghastly?'

'Because nothing should be called a camp unless it's a luxury safari hotel in Africa. And Jack stayed there!' she barked back.

After about another kilometre down the road, and away from the main part of the strip which Lucinda had started to find reassuring thanks to a few decent-looking restaurants and shops, they pulled in and saw a sign surrounded by tealights and with what looked like a pyramid with an eye in the middle of it, saying Camp Mayo.

The driver unloaded their bags on the side of the road and headed back to his seat.

Anthony turned to the four boys, who he took to be French from their conversation, before asking, 'Vous restez ici aussi?'

They responded, 'Non, monsieur, nous campons à proximité sur la plage, mais cet endroit est très cool. Vous vous amuserez' which was beyond Anthony's limited French comprehension, but which he took as roughly meaning, 'No, but this place is cool. You'll have fun.'

A muscular American man in his early 20s, with a baggy-fitting Camp Mayo vest and a blond ponytail arrived by the gate.

'Welcome to Camp Mayo. You must be the Palmers. We've been expecting you,' he winked.

'You must be Leonardo then?' Lucinda said, putting her hand out to shake his.

'No, I'm Gabriel. Leonardo's away for a couple of days, but he told me to look after you.'

'Ah, the Angel Gabriel,' Lucinda said with a forced smile.

'Hello, I'm Anthony Palmer. How do you do? We're pleased to be here,' Anthony said, before Gabriel had a chance to respond to Lucinda.

'I'll get your bags, and then please, follow me,' Gabriel said, picking up the luggage before Anthony could offer to help, and carrying it on his back through their entrance gate with some rather impressive biceps on full display.

Once they were through the gate and had signed in at what was allegedly a reception hut, they were able to look onto the rest of the camp.

There were no buildings, only a selection of yurts and wooden structures built into the sand dunes, with everything lit up by candle lanterns liberally positioned around the camp.

Over the dunes, you could hear the soft beat of music playing. Lucinda rolled her eyes before agreeing with Anthony that, rather than sounding intrusive and disturbing, the music had an almost reassuring hypnotic rhythm to it.

'I'll take you to your sanctuary now, Mr and Mrs Palmer,' Gabriel said. 'Come this way, but please first remove your shoes. We operate a fully barefoot policy here; that's probably our only rule.'

With some difficulty, they both removed their shoes and followed Gabriel through to their yurt.

'Welcome to your home for the next week. Is there anything else I can get you for now?'

'No, thank you, Gabriel. All I need is a bed! It's been a long day,' Lucinda replied.

'In which case, I'll see you tomorrow and we can work out your schedule for the week. Sleep well.'

Gabriel closed the door behind them and then it was just the two of them in their yurt, which, without the light of the lanterns outside, suddenly seemed rather dark and claustrophobic.

Lucinda was normally meticulous about unpacking her bags and clothes neatly on arrival, but after their journey, she could think of little other than going to sleep. Today's experience had simply confirmed to her that she actually loathed travelling, particularly when exhausting stopovers were included.

Beforehand, though, she would find the light source, use the bathroom and brush her teeth. Using the light from Anthony's phone, she managed to find a torch by the side of her bed, which she turned on and shone expectantly around the room.

'Anthony, where's the bathroom in this bloody place?' she snapped, having only spotted that the only door to the yurt was the one through which they had just entered.

'Do you know, I wondered that too, Lucinda. I'm afraid I don't think we have one. Must be outside,' he suggested cautiously, not wanting to unleash further scolding from his wife.

'Outside? What do you mean, outside? For fuck's sake, Jack,' Lucinda sighed, before continuing her rant at

Anthony. 'Well, I need to use it, so you'd better come with me right now and hold the torch. Otherwise, no doubt, I'll end up stepping on a scorpion and that will probably be the end of me,' before crossly muttering to herself afterwards, 'perhaps preferable to a week of *this* place.'

The two of them walked out of their yurt and towards the main communal area, which still seemed suspiciously quiet. Using the light of the lantern, Anthony was able to guide them towards a wooden sign they had noticed earlier, indicating the "washrooms".

The washroom was less of a room and more of a canvas structure which, like most things at Camp Mayo, was covered in fairy lights and had a beaded curtain made of shells as an entrance. Inside, there were four sinks and two cubicles, again with shell curtains as doors. The smell of incense was so strong, it overpowered any natural odours.

'Shine the bloody torch this way so I can at least see what I'm doing in this ghastly little set-up,' Lucinda demanded.

Anthony obligingly shone the torch towards a cubicle and waited until Lucinda had finished. She then brushed her teeth in the sink and washed her hands, before charging out of the structure as quickly as she could as Anthony scampered after her to illuminate her way.

Back in the yurt, she changed into her pyjamas and lowered herself to the mattress on the floor. She indulged herself with thoughts of self-pity, but not for long, as it was less than a minute before she fell into a deep and much-needed sleep. Anthony waited until he was absolutely sure that she was asleep before carefully picking up the torch and tiptoeing back to the bathroom. Exhausted himself, he retraced their steps and walked straight back through the curtain of shells to the washroom and headed towards the lavatory cubicles inside.

But on pulling back the second curtain, to his surprise, he saw a woman sitting down on the loo staring straight back at him. She was wearing a green one-piece jumpsuit, requiring her to have rolled the whole garment down from the top. This left her bare breasts exposed, between which a gold pendant hung, gently swaying between her cleavage. Anthony knew he should avert his eyes immediately, but allowed himself to stare at the woman for longer than in any other normal scenario he would have deemed gentlemanly. After a couple of seconds, the very limit of what he felt could be perceived as accidental, he turned his head.

'God, sorry! Shit! I really am so sorry. It didn't occur to me that anyone would be in here,' he blurted embarrassedly.

'Don't worry. My fault entirely. I should have said something when you came into the washroom. Decided against it. Oops,' the woman responded confidently with her American accent.

'Oh, erm, I'll come back later then, shall I? Don't worry!' said Anthony, before deciding that the best option was to scurry out of the canvas tent even more quickly than he had entered.

In his effort to make a swift exit, Anthony stepped backwards onto the wooden block of incense that had been burning away by the door, sending a shooting pain straight to his left foot. 'Owww!' he yelped. 'Buggeration! Bloody hell, so unbelievably sorry,' he said again to the woman on the loo. 'I've just burnt myself and now knocked over the incense pot. Silly me!' He bent down to straighten things up, before pausing as he realised that he was now on his hands and knees, right in front of the woman on the loo.

'You know what? I'll just go now. Probably best. Sorry.'

Not wanting to be seen lingering outside the washroom holding his foot, nor choosing to go back to his yurt and face waking up Lucinda, he instead walked towards the sound of the sea and the music which he could still hear nearby.

He hadn't realised initially just how close to the sea they were. The waves gently rolled in against the sand on the other side of the dunes.

About 20 yards to his right, a small group of people, each dressed like exotic hippies wearing Mexican kaftans over their swimwear were huddled around a campfire. One of them was strumming a guitar, while another accompanied him on a drum. He couldn't be sure, but it looked like Gabriel on the guitar, and he assumed those with him were others working in Tulum for the season, rather than guests.

Anthony sat down on the beach and let the waves gently break against his burnt foot in an effort to soothe the stinging pain from when he stepped on the incense block. Although the water was probably too warm to do much good, the sensation of the waves against his skin diverted his mind from the wound.

About 500 metres further down the beach, back towards the strip they had driven through on their way to the camp, he could see flashing lights and heard what he recognised to be electronic music.

He took it all in, and by the time he checked his watch, he realised he must have been sat there for at least fifteen minutes. Surely by now the coast would be clear to the bathroom? He didn't want to take any more chances so sat for another couple of minutes before dusting the sand off his legs and heading back over the dunes the way he had come from the camp.

This time when he got back to the washrooms, he waited outside for a moment. Realising there was only canvas to knock against, he instead began whispering quietly, 'Hello. Hello…?' just to be sure they weren't occupied.

If anyone had seen him standing on one leg and talking to the canvas wall, they would have probably assumed he was high on something; fortunately, they did not.

He took a deep breath and stepped back into the scene of his earlier embarrassment, being careful to ensure his feet were where they should be. The incense block had been picked up and relit with fresh sticks.

Five minutes later, he was back in the yurt and quietly slipped into bed next to Lucinda, who had remained fast asleep, thank God.

Despite the long journey and his weariness, Anthony found he couldn't sleep. Instead, he lay on the bed, with his eyes open, staring up at the exposed wooden structure of their yurt above him. In his head, he recounted the evening's developments over and over again, but each time it got to the stage of opening the canvas washroom door to reveal the mysterious woman sat on the loo, he would pause with the image of her breasts in his head. Anthony wasn't one for internet porn or smutty magazines, unlike some of his colleagues who he knew watched it habitually. In fact, the only bare breasts he had laid eyes upon for as long as he could remember had been Lucinda's, and that had become a seriously infrequent occurrence.

Lucinda had long stopped considering her breasts to be something of sexual desire. Rather, she saw her buxom chest as a physical inconvenience, and any thoughts she might have once had of enticing Anthony, or anyone for that matter, to bed with her were now distant history.

But there was something about the situation that Anthony had witnessed which awoke senses deep inside him that he had rather forgotten existed. It couldn't have been the size of her breasts that caused this, for they were by no means large. But they were perfectly round, as if they had been cast with the mould of a pudding bowl, he mused, with the tips of her nipples upturned. Unable to get the image out of his head, Anthony finally drifted off to sleep.

*

As the sun rose the following morning, the yurt filled with natural light, revealing the full simplicity of its structure. It was 6am, but with the combination of light and jetlag, there was little chance of them going back to sleep.

There were a couple of small armchairs in the corner of the room, with a miniature rustic wooden trunk between them, doubling up as a coffee table. On the other side of the bed was a wooden clothes rail, a small chest of drawers and a shoe rack. Lucinda didn't quite understand why such a significant proportion of the little valuable space they had inside the yurt was taken up with the shoe rack, given that footwear was seemingly prohibited.

Next to the entrance door there was also a wood burner, which might have been useful if their yurt was in Mongolia, where yurts had originated from, but had limited use on the Caribbean Sea, where the temperature stayed fairly consistently warm throughout the year.

Despite its simplicity, Lucinda was surprised by the comfort of the bed and had enjoyed the best night's sleep for as long as she could remember. Anthony was enjoying the morning peace, broken only by birdsong and the sound of the waves in the distance, when a re-energised Lucinda piped up,

'Come on, Anthony. Chop, chop! I need the bathroom; will you grab my stuff and come with me?'

'You realise it *is* light outside now, Lucinda? You're probably not in need of a torch now, darling.'

'Yes, thank you, I'd worked that out myself. Just come with me, though. I don't know what on earth's out there.'

They put on their linen dressing gowns that had been left out for them on the clothes rail, a fairly civilised touch, thought Lucinda with raised eyebrows, and headed back to the washroom. By their door, they were also grateful to find a fresh pot of coffee, two mugs and a plate of freshly baked croissants, which Anthony carefully placed on the little table outside the yurt.

Once they returned from the washroom, which Lucinda realised was neither as far nor unpleasant as she had remembered it being, they enjoyed their breakfast listening to the sounds of the circling swifts flying above them from tree to tree.

Lucinda felt grateful for the birds' presence as it gave them something to focus on, and distracted them both from the increasingly awkward silence she felt between them.

These moments could be avoided at Ferryman's Cottage, for there was always something to keep them busy, and it was rare that they ever found themselves alone with nothing to do other than make conversation.

But here, sitting outside their yurt in Mexico, that stark reality was staring them straight in the face. After twenty-two years of marriage, they had quite literally run out of things to say to each other. Eventually, the silence was broken, by Anthony.

'Isn't that sound of the waves breaking the most lovely thing to wake up to?' Anthony said congenially.

'Yes, I suppose it is,' Lucinda replied. *One week, that's all. One more week*, she thought to herself.

They heard a male voice cough before Gabriel appeared around the side of the yurt. He seemed to be wearing some sort of white toga outfit, once again revealing his arms which they could now see were completely covered in Celtic tattoos.

'How did everyone sleep?' he asked, and without giving Lucinda or Anthony a chance to respond, proceeded to answer his own question. 'That's great, great. So, I wanted to come and give thanks for the day ahead with you guys and help us think about the plans that await you over the next week or so. Perhaps I could tell you a little about what we've got going on here; you can let me know what you would like to join, and I'll also let you know a bit about what else you can do here in Tulum. Does that sound good?'

Again, before either of them was able to answer, Gabriel motored on.

'That's great. So, each morning at 8am, we do our sanctum yoga classes just here on the beach in front of us. They're beautiful, and a wonderful way for you to reach inner peace through a voyage of self-discovery. Then in the evenings, around 6pm, we do our themed yoga classes here too. These alternate between Vinyasa, Drum and Tantric classes. We also do a prenatal one, if you're interested.'

'Thank you. I'm not. I'm fifty-eight,' replied Lucinda, somewhat bemused.

'No, sure, great. I just wanted to let you know we offer that too.' The irony had been lost on Gabriel.

'What's the drum yoga class about?' Anthony asked.

'It's when we use the beat of a drum to generate deep meditative experiences.'

'I see. Perfect. That sounds lovely. Perfect. Great. Thank you,' Anthony said, leaving Gabriel wondering if the Brit had an incredibly polite form of Tourette's.

'We also have our beach evenings on Wednesdays and Fridays, when we encourage all our guests to come together for group dances under the stars. We try and keep these as private occasions for our guests; very different from the raves you'll find further down the beach. You probably thought it was pretty quiet last night? That's because it was Monday. Wednesdays, Thursdays, Fridays and Saturdays are the big nights here. You're gonna love it.'

'Sounds heavenly,' Lucinda responded, barely able to accompany her comment with an equally sarcastic smile.

'Awesome. I'm so pleased to hear you guys are stoked for this,' answered Gabriel.

'And what about the trips to see the ruins, or any boat trips perhaps?' Anthony asked.

'Oh yeah, we do that too. There is the fishing man and the ruin man. I just, like, call them and they come and get you. Easy as that. When d'you wanna go?'

'Well, shall we go this morning? Lucinda, what do you think, darling?'

'Why not? Let's give it a try.'

'Right, I'll call the ruin man now. Have a great day, guys, and don't forget to give thanks.'

'Thanks,' they replied in unison.

*

Twenty minutes later, they were in a cab on their way to the Mayan ruins on the edge of town that dated back to AD 564. The benefit of getting there early in the day meant they had the whole place almost to themselves, but even at that time, Lucinda found the heat intolerable.

The Tulum ruins, built on top of a cliff, had once been a bustling Mayan port and home to over 600 people, with dwellings and scattered stones positioned around a central area of grass.

'These Mayans seemed rather more advanced in their accommodation than we seem to be at Camp Mayo today,' joked Anthony. 'Look here, this one even has a stone toilet attached to its house.' Lucinda gave a little smirk from the corner of her mouth.

The Mayan town had been built around a prominent castle and temple, and some of the inside walls still possessed original murals, which had been surprisingly well preserved.

After forty-five minutes of exploring the different Mayan buildings, the crowds started to build up and the heat became too much; they decided it was time to head on. Back at the entrance, Mr Ruin Man, their driver, was waiting under a tree with four other drivers who he clearly knew well.

'You like?' Mr Ruin Man asked, as he jumped up to greet them.

'Very much, yes, but too hot now!' Lucinda responded.

'You want to go swimming to cool off? I know a secret place, the best *cenote* around. No tourists.'

This part of Mexico was known for its *cenotes*, a series of natural swimming pools scattered around the jungle, formed when the natural limestone bedrock had collapsed over the years, leaving perfect freshwater pools behind.

Anthony had read about them and was keen to visit, so he asked Lucinda if she was happy to go. He had brought a beach bag with them, just in case they had wanted to stop and swim on the way home, and so were fully equipped for the excursion anyway.

'Sure. It's not like there's that much to do back at the camp, is there? Let's go,' Lucinda said, and they got back in the car.

Ten minutes later, Mr Ruin Man pulled into a petrol station, off the main road. Anthony and Lucinda assumed this was for a petrol top-up, but when he pulled in on the far side of the forecourt away from the pumps, they both looked a little confused.

Putting his hands upside down to his face, as if imitating a pair of glasses, Mr Ruin Man said in one of his evidently well-practised English phrases, 'You buy! You buy!'

Lucinda initially assumed he wanted them to pay for his petrol, before crossly turning to Anthony with a "told you so" sort of face and saying, 'They're always trying to get something, aren't they? Always wanting more.'

'Who are?' Anthony asked, somewhat confused.

'These people, the Mexicans. Isn't it enough that we've already paid well over the odds to drive us this morning? Now he wants us to pay for his petrol too. I won't have it. Let's tell him to take us back to the hotel, right now.'

From the front seat, Mr Ruin Man continued mimicking his glasses on his face, saying louder, 'You *must* buy! Here, you buy!' He then made a swimming gesture, at which point Anthony clicked.

'Ahh! I think he means we need to buy a snorkelling mask! What a thoughtful man,' Anthony said.

'Yes, yes! You snorkel!' Mr Ruin Man said, satisfied that they had finally understood him.

Anthony got out of the car and walked into the petrol station shop, soon finding a large basket marked "cenote snorkel" on the side. He picked up two boxes of snorkels from the basket, one large, one medium, and handed the shop assistant 400 pesos, about $15. Back in the car, Lucinda and Mr Ruin Man were sat in uncomfortable silence.

Ten minutes later, they were slowly navigating the little white Hyundai around potholes along a jungle track.

'Nearly arrive, you see, no tourists here. Not far, not far!' Mr Ruin Man said over the front seat, in an effort to reassure them as he sensed Lucinda's increasing unease.

They eventually arrived at a road barrier, where he pulled over and parked next to two other white Hyundai taxis. They got out of the car, and Mr Ruin Man pointed down a path off to their left, where there were three hotel rental bicycles leaning against a tree. They both found the presence of others here in the middle of the jungle reassuring.

About 50 metres down the path, they found a small table with an elderly Mexican man sat behind it and a sign saying 200 pesos. Anthony handed over some notes from his pocket and in exchange received a couple of towels.

They followed the path on for about 75 metres further when they heard splashes. And then, in front of them, they saw the rock pool and its crystal clear water, below overhanging rocks and tropical trees and flowers. It was unquestionably one of the most magical swimming spots either of them had seen before.

On their right, two heavily oiled men were sunbathing together on a rock. It was only after putting on his prescription sunglasses that it occurred to Anthony that the men were completely naked, with the younger of the two possessing a penis that wouldn't have been much smaller than a woman's arm. Surely it must be a health hazard having something that size dangling around, he thought to himself.

It was an easy decision, therefore, to walk down the path on the left instead, which led to another rock and a large branch growing out over the water about six feet below, to which someone had attached a swing rope.

As they changed into their swimwear, Anthony held up a towel to provide Lucinda with some screening, not that it seemed to be required. As they were doing this, another German couple walked past, also naked. Anthony recognised them as the couple from the airport minibus who checked into the naturist hotel. They nodded at each other and casually strode on to the other side of the *cenote*.

'Why is everyone here naked?' Lucinda whispered to Anthony, trying not to laugh.

'God knows! Isn't it enough for these people to be naked at their own naturist hotels? Shall we go for it?'

'Go for what precisely, Anthony?'

'You know; no costumes. Otherwise, we might look a little silly while everyone else is stark bollock naked!' Anthony reasoned.

'Not nearly as silly as we look without them. Now hold that towel up higher!'

Swimwear on, they jumped off the rock and into the clear water below. As they momentarily escaped the humidity of the day and washed off the salt from their bodies, they felt refreshed.

They had, of course, heard about the healing quality of minerals and knew there were many specialists who swore by the power of crystals and healing salts, but neither of them had given this much thought in the past. There had been no reason to. However, on entering the rock pool, they felt that the water was turbocharging their energy and re-purifying their lethargic bodies. It was as if they had taken a double shot of life.

Once Lucinda had resurfaced in the water, which was surprisingly cool, she took a deep breath and followed the rock face down under the water, feeling the roughness of its surface that had stood unchanged for thousands of years.

The rock had a solidity to its presence. Solidity: something that she felt her life had lacked for as long as she could remember. For the first time since her days at Ladbroke Walk, Lucinda felt an overwhelming presence of her first husband and her only true love, David.

She held her breath tight and continued to swim deeper into the rock pool, with one hand guiding her way on the stone. With her eyes closed, she stroked the rock as if it was the face of her late husband, in the way she remembered doing each morning that she woke up next to him. She began to feel her lungs burning but couldn't quite bring herself to withdraw from her embrace with the rock; her embrace with David. She rested her forehead against him and allowed herself to be comforted as she had been before. Finally, her body starved of oxygen could take no more, and she allowed herself to drift back up towards the surface. She felt she was losing him all over again. With one final kick with her legs, she propelled herself back to the present day.

When she opened her eyes, she immediately burst into tears. Anthony, who had been floating on his back in pretty much the same spot throughout her ordeal, hadn't even noticed that Lucinda had been under the water for so long.

Anthony heard her cries before he saw her. Assuming she had been stung by a jellyfish or had crashed herself against a rock, he quickly swam over towards her.

'Lucinda! Lucinda, what's wrong, darling? What's wrong?' he called out to her.

But her cries had become louder and more uncontrollable. By the time Anthony reached her, tears were streaming down her face, and she was struggling to take in enough oxygen before the next round of cries came out again.

'Please just get off me, Anthony. I'm fine. Just leave me. Will you, please?' Lucinda managed to say between her sobs.

'C'mon, let's get you out of the water. Let's head back, shall we?' Anthony said, trying to comfort her.

'No, please, Anthony. I just want to be here, in the water, alone for a bit. Can you please just give me that?'

Her cries had caused understandable concern amongst the other swimmers, who had now come over to see what was happening.

'Everything okay there, sir?' came an American voice above him.

Anthony glanced up to the rock to see the younger oiled man, looking down at him accusingly.

'I said everything okay? Can I help with anything?' the man repeated.

'God, no,' Anthony responded, before realising he sounded too curt. 'Sorry. No. I mean, we're fine, she's fine; just hit her foot on the wall, didn't you, darling, that's all. But thank you.'

Lucinda's sobs had finally receded, and she was starting to feel embarrassed.

'I'll just go for a swim, shall I, Lucinda? I'll see you back here then, if you're sure you're okay.'

Lucinda nodded, feeling slightly embarrassed by her outburst, as Anthony breaststroked himself towards the other side of the rock pool, wondering what on earth had just happened.

She knew that Anthony didn't have a bad bone in his body, but also that there was nothing he could do to change the way she felt, or didn't feel, about him. But if her experience under the water taught her anything, then it was that she hadn't been honest with herself, and it had been going on for too long now.

Since David's death, she had kept any emotions she had compressed inside her, like propane squeezed into a gas canister; only her body was the canister, and with age, the volume it could accommodate was decreasing year by year.

Finally, she was finding the courage to be honest with herself. Every part of her was still devoted to her late husband. She realised now that she had never truly grieved his death. Her immediate priority after David's accident was to secure her children's future. To do everything she could to give them the upbringing that they would have had if David were still around. Anthony was part of that. He was a component in the life she was trying to build, a life that allowed her to protect her children.

At the moment that David's life support machine had been switched off, she knew that she had stopped living for herself. She had taken herself out of the equation. But as she sacrificed her life for the sake of her children, she denied Anthony his chance of happiness too.

For she realised now that she'd never given him a chance. Her children were now grown up and had their own lives ahead of them. Sophie was starting a new life with Harry up in Angus, and although Jack had not had a serious girlfriend since Bells, who he dated during his first year of Newcastle University, Lucinda knew he would be fine. Jack was always fine.

She recognised at that moment that her duties as a mother, raising her children, were complete. She had done everything she could, and now they were on their own.

But what about her life now? This must be the time to start it again, a fresh beginning. She missed David dearly and had done every day since that dreadful accident. She no longer needed to hide that from the world. She would treasure his memory and vowed to think and talk about him more going forward. It was ridiculous, she felt, to have talked about him so rarely. Not to Anthony, not to her friends, and not even her children, beyond the few stories she had recounted when they were younger and has asked about their father. That would change. By never even telling Anthony how much David had meant to her, and how she still felt, she realised she had never given him the chance to be his own person. She had never even considered what kind of man was hidden there, beneath the rather awkward introvert that had been in the background of her life for the last twenty-two years.

Like a plant cutting that had been kept out of the light, he had never had the opportunity to grow. Whether Anthony's malnourished buds did have the ability to blossom was another matter, but she at least wanted to give him the chance of experiencing that light. She would give him that, she told herself. She owed that to him.

But first, she wanted to see David one more time. After taking a deep breath, she swam back beneath the surface holding the steadfast rock wall beneath her. She embraced the rock beneath the surface with arms outstretched, while placing her lips upon a piece of jagged limestone on the edge. 'I love you, David. I always will,' she mouthed to the rock face. And after one final stroke of the rock, she swam back to the surface to go and find her husband.

*

Anthony, unsure of what was going on with Lucinda, had swam around the corner of the *cenote*, only to find that it expanded into an even more dramatic rock pool, which meandered its way through various boulders, creating a network of channels and private spaces. With his newly purchased snorkelling equipment now on, he followed the water through a sunken archway between two large rocks, and into a split. One fork linked the channel back to the main rock pool, and the second route was less clear, but he decided to follow it anyway. After a few metres, it opened up into a private area with large slabs of partially submerged limestone, and perfect for sunbathing. Like a frog who had discovered a fresh lily pad, Anthony made himself comfortable against the smooth rock, with his toes in the water. He put his head back on the rock, closed his eyes and began to daydream.

It didn't take long for his mind to dart back to the woman in the green jumpsuit and her bare, round breasts. The confidence with which she nonchalantly spoke to him, making no effort to cover herself. It wasn't something he had really come across before.

Anthony had only had one girlfriend before Lucinda and had never really been into sex. It had always been a rather messy old business in his eyes, and so he'd never really given it much thought. But what was it about that woman, he questioned, that he found so difficult to shake off?

Perhaps there was simply a voyeuristic excitement to the whole episode that was new to him. Or was it technically voyeuristic? he wondered, as that would suggest he had been watching her without her knowledge. She certainly knew he was looking at her and had done absolutely nothing to conceal herself. That was different.

Before he could give the whole experience any more thought, Lucinda appeared on the rock next to him.

'There you are, Anthony. I've been swimming about for ages trying to find you. Did you fall asleep?' she asked, not unkindly. It turned out that he had. 'I was worried about where you'd got to. Thought those nice boys with their oiled bodies might have taken you off with them!'

'Ha, no, just here. On my rock. Nice place this, isn't it? Are you feeling better now?' Anthony asked with genuine concern.

'Yes, dear. Thank you.' Lucinda leant forward and kissed Anthony softly on the cheek. 'Really, thank you. For everything.'

'Right. Well, sure,' Anthony mumbled, without really knowing what she was thanking him for.

'Should get going, I guess. Think our driver will be worried if we're much longer. I suggest we head back to the hotel, I mean, camp, and park ourselves on the beach for the afternoon, with a cold bottle of wine.'

- Chapter Eight -

Camp Mayo, Tulum

By the time they arrived back at the camp, it was nearly 2pm. After the morning's activities and having only had a croissant for breakfast, they were both starving and ready for lunch.

'Why don't we wander down to the beach and try that nice restaurant, at the hotel where we dropped the couple from the minibus?' Lucinda suggested.

'Perfect plan,' Anthony agreed.

Back in the room they changed their clothes, Anthony got his wallet and his now rather battered, but wonderfully personalised, Panama hat, and they headed out over the dunes towards the beach. The restaurant was about a kilometre down the beach, back towards the centre of town.

From the beach, you could appreciate how sympathetically the hotels and guesthouses had been developed along the stretch, so in keeping with the natural landscape, unlike so many beach resorts these days. From the road, you hardly knew anything was there at all, but from the coast, you could just catch glimpses of the different hotels, all of which had been intertwined with their surroundings of sand dunes and palm trees to create an almost continuous development of boutique hotels, each one probably accommodating no more than thirty guests.

Lucinda and Anthony soon realised that there was no way they were going to be able to spot the particular hotel they had in mind from the beach, so after a short while, they decided to stop at one they liked the look of. It was called 2BE Tulum and had a chic beachfront bar with a collection of rattan furniture spilling out onto the sand.

The chef was cooking freshly caught fish over an open grill under a palm tree, with a number of stylish couples settling down to various seafood platters and magnum bottles of AIX rosé. Lucinda knew this particular brand because it was always what Sophie brought with her when she came to stay during the summer. The magnums were deceptive. Although they looked intimidatingly large when put in an ice bucket on a lunch table, they had a pesky habit of always ending up empty far sooner than you would expect. Lucinda felt confident they could take one on, having felt in need of a drink ever since she emerged from her first dive into the rock pool that morning.

They walked hesitantly towards one of the empty tables, a few feet back from the chef. On the next table sat a beautiful dark-haired girl, who couldn't have been much older than twenty, with Sanskrit writing tattooed up her left arm and a black bikini that barely contained her bust. Opposite her was an American man with his blue baseball cap back to front, a tight navy V-necked t-shirt, emphasising his bulging biceps. They looked like they could have been the stars of a Hollywood porn movie, Lucinda thought. But now looking around the other tables in the restaurant, Lucinda realised that their attire was seemingly the unofficial dress code.

For the first time since she was a teenager going to one of her coolest friend's 18th birthday parties, Lucinda felt uncomfortably self-conscious about her own attire. In a moment of panic, she turned around and went to grab Anthony's arm to return to the beach and find an alternative venue for lunch. But before she could do so, a tall Frenchman, with tight green shorts, white pumps without socks, and white polo shirt saying 2BE Tulum, greeted her.

'Welcome to 2BE Tulum. If you would like to follow me just this way, I have a nice table for two for you for lunch.' The waiter then led them back to the table Lucinda had been hovering over only moments earlier, and seated them right next to the adult movie stars. The waiter handed them two menus. 'And can I get you a drink for now?' he asked.

Without a moment's hesitation, Lucinda responded. 'Yes, rosé wine, please. A bottle.'

Anthony looked up and nodded approvingly.

'Any particular wine? The list is at the back of the menu,' the waiter added.

'A very cold bottle of AIX, please,' Lucinda replied. Lucinda loved wine. All wine, in fact, but particularly cold rosé, or a crisp Sauvignon Blanc for lunch on a hot day. Part of the appeal of going to spend time with her cousin at their wine farm in South Africa, other than starting a new life for herself, was to surround herself with delicious wine. If she couldn't surround herself with people she loved, then wine would make a sufficient alternative.

She was quite strict with herself, though. At home, she would always try and give herself two days a week on which she wouldn't drink, and she wouldn't touch a drop during the day, apart from on a weekend. But when she was on holiday, as she was now, if you could call it that, she wasn't going to hold back.

When the waiter returned with their bottle, she ignored his offer of tasting the wine first. 'I'm sure it's fine,' she said, gesturing to him to go ahead and pour both glasses. He did so, and left the bottle in an ice bucket by the side of their table.

Over Anthony's shoulder, she watched the dark-haired girl playing on her phone, while her boyfriend seemed to be watching the movements of a seagull near them trying to eat a stray chip from an empty plate left on a sun bed, without getting caught by its now dozing owner.

She must be Instagramming, Lucinda thought. That's all young people do these days, she had been told. It was certainly worthy of an Instagram shot, she thought, as she glanced, feeling like she could be in a mirror maze with almost identically dressed beautiful couples at every table.

She glanced down at her own clothes and as she did, she felt slightly appalled with herself for even thinking like this. She was far too old and wise to be influenced by such trivial concerns as her clothes. But she couldn't quite help a little self-doubt creeping in.

Her blue linen shirt had a small rip under her left arm and a selection of gardening stains on the bottom. Her khaki shorts, she realised, were an old pair of Jack's she had inherited from him a few years back, and her blue deck shoes were the same pair she had bought in Burnham Market four years ago, with the left sole now starting to detach from the rest of the shoe.

Lucinda had never really shown any interest in clothes, even in her Savills days, when all the other women in the office effectively wore the same thing; a short (sometimes alarmingly so) navy blue skirt, a tight white shirt, normally with one button too many left undone, a pearl necklace and knee-high dark suede boots. Now she tended to just live in her Wellington boots at home, her jeans, a couple of shirts and, if it was cold, a jacket. She hadn't even given much thought to her holiday wardrobe, but now she wished she had at least *something* a little less old and frumpy.

After a large gulp of her wine, which tasted just as she had hoped it would, she took herself to the bathroom.

Another waiter, who was as equally handsome as the first, directed her towards a separate building, where a bamboo door led to a concrete washroom. Unlike their own at Camp Mayo, Lucinda was relieved that this one had walls, doors and reliable hot water.

In front of the mirror, she looked at herself again. She knew she was still in reasonable shape for her age, thanks to all the walking she did having done her good. But she realised she just looked like she had stopped, well, trying.

She had noticed that one of the women at the restaurant wore her shirt undone and tied into a knot at the front. Lucinda tried that in front of the mirror. At first, she tied it too low, revealing her nude Marks and Spencer bra.

She tried again, only this time with the knot halfway up her shirt. Still it certainly focussed attention towards her cleavage but was more than passable. Lucinda's breasts were still in good shape, and the knot reinforced that, giving them additional uplift.

She tightened the knot slightly and rolled up the ends of her shorts, improving their shape sufficiently. As she tucked the back of the shirt into her shorts, which also had the added benefit of hiding the stains at the bottom, the man on the table behind her, in the V-necked t-shirt walked into the lavatory. He nodded at Lucinda briskly then walked into the cubicle behind her. What was he thinking walking into the women's loo? Lucinda thought as she walked out to double-check the sign on the door. *Restroom* was all it said, which she realised meant unisex.

She sat back down at the table and poured herself another glass of wine.

'I took a punt, Lucinda, and ordered you the grilled fish of the day. Hope that's okay?' Anthony said from across the table. He didn't like waiting when it came to ordering. After years of Lucinda's indecisiveness when it came to ordering food, he had one day just taken control of the situation, and it had mostly worked out fine.

'Perfect,' Lucinda smiled back, trying to work out whether Anthony had noticed the change in her shirt. She knew his facial expressions pretty well, she thought, and reading the glance he gave her, she took it to mean: *Lucinda looks slightly different, but I can't for the life of me think what it is.* He had noticed something, though, and that was a start.

The rosé, as expected, had done its usual trick of magically disappearing from the bottle rather sooner than they might have originally thought. The grilled fish was yet to arrive, but rather than going for the second bottle, Anthony, who was as guilty as Lucinda when it came to fast wine consumption, suggested they went for some margaritas instead, particularly as they were listed as the 2BE Tulum's cocktail speciality.

The wine had tempered any lingering concerns Lucinda had about her outfit, and once the margaritas hit them, she found herself more relaxed than she could remember in a long time. The grilled fish was the most delicious she had ever tasted, and she felt her spirits lifting.

Once they had finished their main courses, they moved to a pair of oversized grey beanbags that were positioned in front of the bar on the beach. After ordering two more margaritas, they lay back on the beanbags listening to the sound of the waves in front of them, and the gentle music from the bar behind.

Before long, Anthony was asleep, dozing to the lazily paced house music. The last time Lucinda could remember lying on a foreign beach with Anthony was their honeymoon to Corfu, six months after their wedding. They decided, or rather Lucinda decided, it made more sense to bring Sophie and Jack with them, so rather than a romantic break it turned into more of a family holiday. Diana and Andrew, when he was still alive, had a three-bedroom villa on the edge of a cliff, overlooking a beautiful secluded cove on the west side of the island, and which they had been given for a week as a wedding present.

Their wedding had been efficient in its preparation and swift in its execution. Chelsea Registry Office on the King's Road, followed by lunch for ten at Oriel on Sloane Square, before it changed hands due to an unaffordable hike in rent.

She had slept with Andrew only twice before their wedding. Once quite soon after meeting him, when she stayed over at the flat he used to own in Battersea, overlooking the river. They had both drunk too much, after having spent the evening at a friend's fortieth birthday party.

The second time was the following morning, after he had gone out to the supermarket to try and buy her some breakfast but made such a mess of the omelette, twice, that she'd told him to give up and come back to bed. Both times had been fleeting, without Lucinda giving it much of a thought.

With David, she used to think of their sex as passionate, and sensed a deep connection of two bodies and souls. Even when it was just a rushed fuck after work and before they had to be at a dinner, it was always more than just sex with David. She hadn't had that same feeling with anyone since David had died. It wasn't just Anthony. It was the same with all of the men she had been with after David, which wasn't many; three perhaps.

Once they had arrived in Corfu, Lucinda had wondered if there might have been some additional intimate spark generated in their sex life, simply through being husband and wife. But having the children with them put any thought of that to an end.

It was a strangely polite, slightly awkward embrace, and once the precedent had been set on their honeymoon, it had remained in place ever since.

Lucinda realised then, looking back on when they first started dating each other, that by showing such indifference towards the intimate side of their relationship, the rest of it never had a chance. She had set them off on a downward slope from the start, and Anthony had just adapted accordingly, as men often did.

She remembered back to when they had first met, on that afternoon at Fakenham Racecourse, and when the rain had started pouring down. Despite grinning through the downpour and layering up with several layers of jackets, after just forty minutes of battling with inside-out umbrellas, they decided to call it a day, heading back to the car park.

Anthony had held an umbrella over Lucinda's head, protecting her further from the gusts of wind by using his left hand to force the umbrella down. Less comfortable for Anthony, admittedly, with the water running straight off one side of the umbrella onto his head as a result, while the wind blew full throttle into his face.

Lucinda remembered how chivalrous she thought he was at the time, if not a little barmy. Once she was safely in the car, with him standing outside the window in the rain, she realised that he was still talking after she had closed the door. She wound down her window a fraction to say thank you. By this point, Anthony was almost shouting over the howling rain, trying to say, 'Could I have your number?' But by the time Lucinda finally recognised he was trying to talk, his efforts had resorted to simply shouting, 'Number! Number!' at the top of his voice, to the slight bemusement of the young family trying to get into the car behind them.

Once she finally heard him, she laughed to herself at the sight in front of her: what looked like a madman, screaming at her in the rain outside her window, demanding her telephone number. She wrote it down on a piece of paper and handed it to him through the window. He took it in his wet hand and stuffed it into his only dry trouser pocket.

He waved and headed off to find the others, who were also utterly drenched but in good spirits. Lucinda watched him through the car mirror and felt a fondness for the man she had just met.

It had been so different from her early days with David, when she had been infatuated by every aspect of his life. Anthony was just the friendly accountant with good manners, who started taking the train on the weekends to visit her, initially sleeping in the spare room before the night she invited him into her own.

His entrance into her life had been like simply sticking a pleasing but unexciting extension on a house; there was nothing new, just an additional component. Or perhaps a more accurate comparison, as Lucinda knew only too well, was that Anthony's arrival was like installing a new roof and no longer having to worry about the utility bills.

The longer Lucinda stared at Anthony dozing peacefully on the beanbag, blissfully unaware of his surroundings and the covey of skimpily dressed young people around him, the more she realised how grateful, in fact, she was for his straightforwardness and ease. Nothing seemed to faze him. Before, she worried that this was because he was empty and without substance, which was part of the reason she didn't really think of him as more than just someone with whom she could contentedly cohabit. But now she realised how much she appreciated his simple outlook, and his way of ignoring all of the little things that really didn't matter. Perhaps that's something that comes with age, she wondered. She looked around the beach bar of beautiful people, realising that the last thing she actually really wanted at this stage in her life was to be worrying about how her linen shirt was tied, or how much leg she was showing.

Lucinda leant over from her beanbag and allowed her head to rest gently against Anthony's shoulder. Perhaps it wasn't her relationship with Anthony that was giving her life a feeling of emptiness but instead their rather repetitive and slightly banal daily existence. She knew that she could control that, and perhaps change their outlook on things together, without having to actually change Anthony after all.

When Anthony woke up, he took a swig from the branded glass bottle that had been left out for him by their waiter, and ordered their bill. They walked back to their hotel along the sand, with Lucinda intently observing the different couples, either lying on the sand or walking up and down the beach.

What was going on in their relationships? she wondered to herself. What was it about them that worked together, or was it all just a façade? Did everyone have similar issues? Perhaps that's just the way all relationships are. But then she thought back to David, and the relationship they had. There had never been any compromise, or rationalising to it. It just was.

She looked at a young couple in front of them, running into the sea together and diving through the breaking waves. She hoped they felt what she had once felt. Perhaps she was wrong to try and base everything on that. Should she not be happy that she had experienced that in her life, and now be content with the life she had? After all, she had two wonderful children, a lovely house, enough money to live comfortably and a husband who, despite his shortcomings, was loyal and decent. How lucky she had been to have had that. She took Anthony's hand and squeezed it as they walked the final bit back to their camp.

Neither of them paid any attention to the fact that it was the first time for a number of years that either of them had held each other's hand with any sort of affection.

The rest of the walk didn't take long; the footsteps along the beach of those who had walked before them washed away with the waves, leaving fresh and unbroken sand ahead of them. In the distance, they could see their camp, and for the first time since they arrived, Lucinda was genuinely pleased to be there. *Good old Jack*, she thought.

*

Back at the camp, Gabriel was talking to another identikit man, and when he saw them, he waved and walked over.

'You must be Jack's parents?' the young man grinned.

'Yes, that's us. Hello, I'm Lucinda and this is Anthony.'

She thought best not to point out that although she was Jack's mother, Anthony was instead his stepfather, and Anthony didn't interject either.

'I'm Leonardo,' the young man said. 'We all loved having Jack here; I'm sure you guys are as much fun as he is.'

Lucinda smiled proudly at the thought of her son, and his ability to make friends wherever he went.

'He asked me to make sure you guys have at least one evening at Casa Jaguar restaurant when you're here. Wednesdays and Thursdays are generally the most entertaining there; shall I book you in?'

'Oh, did he? Well, that sounds dangerous! But sure, thanks,' Lucinda said. 'What is it today? Monday? Why not Thursday, then, for our final night?'

'That sounds ideal. And any plans this evening?' Leonardo asked.

'Perhaps just a quiet supper here and an early night. It's been a long day.'

'Brilliant. We'll have dinner delivered to the table outside your yurt, and you guys can chill here then.'

They were just about to move on, when Anthony remembered the morning yoga classes on offer. 'Oh, Gabriel said something about a morning yoga class. Would it be possible to join that tomorrow?'

Lucinda looked bemused. Anthony had never shown any sort of enthusiasm for group exercise, let alone yoga, but rather than find it annoying, which she would have normally done, she saw it as endearing.

'Of course, sure! Just come along to the beach at 8am. It's a beginner's class. Shall I sign you both up?' Leonardo smiled to himself as his mind raced back to the *yoni* massaging class he and Jack had done together before Christmas.

'Certainly not. I'll leave that one for you, Anthony, and I'll have a lie-in with Margaret Atwood.'

Leonardo looked confused.

'She's an author! She means a lie-in with her book. Not actually with another woman. At least I hope not!' Anthony said, just to clarify to Leonardo who was still looking a little confused.

Leonardo nodded. 'Ah yes, of course. Okay, well, enjoy that; and Anthony, we'll see you at 8am. Coffee will be sent to your room at 7am.'

That evening, they had a large sharing plate of freshly caught tiger prawns and a refreshing bottle of Northern California Pinot Noir sent to their yurt. A small campfire had been lit for them, and they sat back and admired the stars above.

- Chapter Nine -
Tulum, Mexico

Anthony had never done yoga before, but he was interested to learn more about it. At his office, Suzi, the HR woman, had approached him about six months ago saying some of the junior members of the team had asked about having the company pay for a yoga instructor to come in in the mornings to give group classes.

Anthony had agreed, suggesting they tried it out for a couple of months to see what the pickup would be, and re-evaluate after that.

Each morning at 7am, a woman called Charlotte would arrive and temporarily transform one of their boardrooms into a yoga studio, where she would then instruct a class for about forty-five minutes.

After two weeks, the classes had become so popular, particularly with the men in the company, that they'd had to move into another boardroom which was twice the size. When that boardroom started filling up too, they capped the number of available places for each class to prevent constant overflow.

Although Anthony had never been to one of the office classes – he felt there was something undignified about a man in his early sixties doing yoga with juniors in his office – he had walked past the boardroom window on a number of occasions and watched the scene of many of his esteemed colleagues wrapping themselves up into all sorts of curious poses.

He thought that trying it out for the first time here in Tulum would give him at least some sense of what all the fuss had been about. He was, after all, the one signing off on the cost of the office yoga classes.

They were woken with a gentle knock on the door at 7am, Gabriel delivering the coffee. Anthony had already been awake when he had knocked; for his entire life, his internal body clock had had a habit of waking him a few moments before his alarm.

He tiptoed out of the door, picking up the running clothes he'd left out the night before to avoid risking waking up Lucinda.

Outside, he got dressed, drank two cups of coffee and then headed back over the dunes to the wooden yoga deck.

He couldn't see any sign of life but realised he was still twenty minutes early. He decided to put his towel and water bottle down on the deck, just so the others knew he was awake and ready, and took himself off for a walk along the beach.

Somewhere in the distance he could hear the sound

of dance music playing, the final tracks of a long night for someone.

Ahead of him was a small group of Americans, probably in their early twenties, evidently on their way home, probably from the source of the distant music. Wherever they were coming from, they seemed in no state for polite conversation with Anthony.

Outside each of the hotels, an army of local hotel workers had suddenly arrived and were busy raking the seaweed that had swept in overnight onto the otherwise pristine white, sandy beaches. With military precision, and with each worker seemingly aware of their hotel's exact boundary, the teams split into two groups; the first team would rake the seaweed into piles, while the second team would be digging large holes in which they buried the amassed algae.

Anthony looked at his watch and turned back towards the camp. When he arrived at the yoga deck, Leonardo had set out five mats. The one for himself at the front of the class had been laid out horizontally, and four others were in vertical pairs behind.

A French couple arrived, who Anthony guessed must be in their early thirties. The woman was dressed in what looked like a rather professional yoga outfit, with fluorescent patterned leggings and a loose maroon vest, and which had *yoga fit* sketched onto the back. He, rather to Anthony's reassurance, was in a pair of baggy swimming shorts and a loose t-shirt. If Anthony had to guess, the woman was an experienced yoga participant who had dragged her husband along to join her while on holiday.

Leonardo asked them all to get comfortable and sit cross-legged while they prepared for the class and waited for the final participant. Anthony rather felt that sitting both comfortably and cross-legged was somewhat of an oxymoron, but rearranged his limbs as best he could.

In the background, Leonardo put on some soft music, which sounded as if it could have been from Tibet, and encouraged everyone to close their eyes and focus on their breathing.

'Deep breaths in, and deep breaths out,' Leonardo called from the front of the class.

Anthony tried to focus on the sequence of his inhale and exhale, but he became distracted by the sound of the final participant, a latecomer, settling themselves on the mat next to him. The softness of their breathing and lightness of their feet suggested it was a woman.

After a few minutes, Leonardo called everyone up to a standing pose and asked the group to stretch their necks as far as they could to the left before holding. Anthony looked out over the beach he had just walked down and was hugely impressed by the speed at which the seaweed had been buried. Then back to face the centre, Leonardo called out, 'And now repeat to the right.'

As Anthony turned his head to the right, he immediately noticed the class latecomer: none other than the woman he had barged into on the lavatory on their first night, with her green jumpsuit rolled down below her waist. The same women whose nipples he had barely stopped thinking about since. Thankfully, she was looking to her right, out along the beach and in the opposite direction from Anthony; otherwise, she would have noticed him almost lose his balance as he felt a rush of adrenalin go through him. He hadn't experienced a feeling like that since he was a young teenager, when the pretty girl in his maths class had smiled at him.

Now completely flustered, he considered taking the opportunity to run away swiftly while the class was looking the other way, before realising that the woman in green would have already noticed him when they had been stretching to the left. Perhaps she hadn't realised it was him? Before he had time to consider his options any further, Leonardo was calling the class back to face the centre.

Not wanting to risk her thinking he was ogling again, Anthony did everything he could to keep his gaze focussed on the ground in front of him. When it was time for another stretch to the right, he would wait for a few seconds to ensure that she would already be looking away from him to avoid catching her eye.

His thoughts remained fixed on the situation throughout the whole class, rather than on the actual yoga itself. He felt like he was in an excruciating *Mr Bean* sketch, rather than on a pathway to spiritual enlightenment. The flip side was the ease with which he was able to admire every aspect of her rear when the woman in green was facing to her right, the pertness of which was emphasised further by her tight yoga leggings.

Her figure was even more desirable than he had remembered. A loo was probably never going to be the most flattering spot for which to admire a female body. But even in the least romantic of settings, Anthony had been taken aback by her athletic figure, and observing her body now in full stretch further reinforced this.

Before the end of the class had even been called, Anthony wondered how he was going to be able to extract himself without having to go through the embarrassment of having to speak to her.

The thought of meeting again, and having to make polite conversation, mostly filled him with dread, though these feelings were undeniably coupled with a small element of excitement too, at the thought of meeting her properly rather than with her squatting on the loo, or stretching her bottom into the air close to his head during her accomplished Downward Dog.

Ultimately, he needn't have worried himself. When the class was called to an end, Leonardo instructed them all to lie on their backs, stretch their legs down as far as they could go, open the palms of their hands and relax until they were ready to start the day.

With the sound of waves behind him, and the gentle music playing from the speakers, Anthony found himself forgetting about the concerns dashing around his head. He let his mind drift off, until he was once again asleep.

He woke to Leonardo whispering next to him, 'Wake up, Anthony', in a tone that suggested he had been repeating this for a little while now.

When he sat up, the rest of the class, including the woman in green, had gone, and their mats had been rolled up at the back of the deck.

'I thought I'd let you doze for a bit,' Leonardo said. 'You were only out for about ten minutes, but it's good for the mind to switch off after our classes.'

'God, sorry about that. And thanks. Feeling good now, I must say. You know, relaxed. I can't believe how quickly the week's passing by.'

'That's what Tulum is for, Anthony. To switch off completely and find parts of yourself that you've buried for many years. It's a release. Just go with it. The earth's calling for you. Mother Nature has her plan for all of us.'

Being unsure of what he was meant to make of Leonardo's words of wisdom, he nodded and muttered something along the lines of, 'Yes. Yes, quite.'

Leonardo rolled up Anthony's yoga mat for him. Anthony thanked him and then headed back towards the yurt. As he reached the sand, Leonardo called out after him, 'Remember, Anthony, throw yourself into your surroundings wholeheartedly. Love Mother Nature. Love yourself.'

Anthony assumed he was just shouting random words at him by the end, but he had enjoyed his yoga class, even if his mind was now racing again at the thought of the woman in green.

When he got to the yurt, he found Lucinda sitting up in bed reading her book. She read all of Margaret Attwood's books. This one was called *Hagseed*, and was about a former theatre director who had reinvented himself as a Shakespeare teacher in one of Canada's toughest male prisons. Not Anthony's choice of holiday reading, but each to their own, he thought.

Lucinda had always read a lot, particularly since Sophie and Jack had been at school. She especially liked novels that had some sort of historical factual element to them, as it allowed her to believe there was an additional educational purpose to reading the book, rather than being purely for pleasure.

'Ah, welcome back, my spiritual guru. Did you find enlightenment, darling?' Lucinda asked, teasing him.

'Well, not quite, but I do feel it's helped me stretch my back out. And I rather fell asleep by mistake at the end.'

'Asleep? Is that what you're meant to be doing? You could have just slept here in the bed. By your standards, I've been doing a morning yoga class too.'

- Chapter Ten -

Glen Clova, Scotland

There was something about the vastness of Glen Clova that Sophie fell in love with straight away. She remembered the first time she went to visit Harry there and was blown away by the dramatic, raw landscape, starting shortly after turning off the A90 on the way out of the increasingly cosmopolitan City of Dundee.

On hitting the lanes off the main road, she found herself being immediately catapulted into open countryside, as they meandered their way down country lanes and crossed babbling brooks. Hidden away in the low ground before reaching the Glens, she just caught sight of the magical castle of Glamis, where the Queen Mother was born, before the lanes and the surrounding scenery gradually gained elevation.

On the higher ground, the open grazing land soon became more dramatic as they left the town of Kirriemuir and headed into the Cairngorms National Park.

The last of the already limited phone signal then disappeared, and the lanes became narrower as the road weaved around and over the cascading rivers coming off the top of the hills above.

On the last turning, signposted towards Glen Clova, Sophie gazed at the basin of the rising jagged rocks and moorland high in the distance. The road, which turned into a track, then ran along the River Clova.

On either side of the road, high up on the rock face, she saw waterfalls cascading down, eventually making their way into the river.

Harry's father, Nigel, had bought the 7,000-acre Brottal Estate after selling his Hertfordshire-based manufacturing business in the 80s. Having always wanted to live surrounded by the Highlands of Scotland, Brottal offered everything he dreamt of, even if his wife, Alison, had been less than enthusiastic initially.

She liked the proximity to London that their comfortable home just outside St Alban's had afforded them, and couldn't understand why Nigel, who she had known since school, now suddenly wanted to pack up and get as far away from London as possible, just when they had all the money they needed to enjoy it. But, like her husband, Alison soon fell in love with Glen Clova and the outdoor lifestyle they had there. And when she did need to go to the city, she found Edinburgh had everything she loved about London, only without quite so many people.

On the farming side, they had sheep and cattle, which more or less looked after themselves, but what Harry was most interested in now was building Brottal as a tourist destination. In the last five years, he had overseen the development of half a dozen self-catering wooden cabins built around the lower woodland area, a few hundred metres from the house and overlooking the river.

The trick was to ensure you could get as many of these cabins in the woods without compromising on the solitude and experience of being immersed in nature that drew people to the area. There was a host of activities for guests to enjoy, but simple, long walks around the surrounding hills proved to be the most popular.

In fact, ever since *Visit Scotland* launched their "Munro Bagging" campaign to bring more visitors to this part of the country, the area had become a popular destination for hill walkers. The term referred to climbing a hill that was higher than 3,000 feet, and of which there were said to be 282 in Scotland. There were three significant Munros in the vicinity of the cabins at Brottal, and a fourth if you included the one upon which Harry had erected a 12-foot viewing platform, just to push the elevation over the 3,000-foot marker.

Those people that successfully summited all 282 Munros called themselves "Munroists", and were granted entry into a highly exclusive hill walking club. Harry never quite understood the mindset of those chasing the Munroist title, but was grateful for their business nonetheless. For him, the landscape could never be considered a challenge to conquer, but instead a privilege to experience. Every time he climbed the hills above his house, he noticed something different about the dramatic landscape. It was just a case of being there, in the moment, that he appreciated so much. Not the head-down focus with which many of the walkers he met took to the hills.

Saturday was handover day, and Sophie walked with Harry around the cabins to check they were all being turned around okay. Seeing the small but comfortable cabins having their sheets changed, she wondered how her mother and stepfather were getting on in their Mexican yurt.

She pulled out her phone and logged on to the cabins' WIFI network – essential for all guests, even those who wanted solitude, Harry would regularly tell her. The "ping, ping, ping" of her WhatsApp notifications came through, the majority of which were for a hen party group she had been added to a couple of months ago. Long since the event, a couple of girls in the group continued to send pictures of their similar-looking dachshund puppies, assuming everyone wanted to be kept up to date with their latest canine activities. Sophie, however, wasn't interested in the slightest as she watched with some irritation as more of the limited data from Brottal WIFI satellite drained away.

*

After they had finished checking the cabins, Harry suggested a walk up the hill behind the house, to catch the sunset coming in. It was a brisk, clear day, and the sun was coming down the valley. From the top of the hill, there was a small bothy hut they regularly liked to visit, from which they had the best view of the setting sun throughout the year.

When they arrived at the hut, Sophie was surprised to find the wood burner was already lit, as if someone had been in there already.

'I thought it might be a bit chilly, so asked Malcolm to get this lit up for us a while ago,' Harry said, sensing Sophie's confusion. Malcolm was one of his farmworkers who managed and maintained the bothies on the estate.

There were a couple of large cashmere blankets that had been woven at a nearby mill used for sitting on the bench on the edge of the hut. Sophie took her usual spot, and Harry wrapped her up in one blanket and used the other one to cover her legs.

Once Sophie was bundled up, Harry went back inside and grabbed the bottle of Pol Roger vintage Champagne he had been saving since it had been given to him for a 21st birthday present, which he had asked Malcolm to hide in the fridge. Next to the bottle there were a couple of silver tankards, which worked well for ensuring its contents stayed cool, as if an evening in Scotland in January hadn't already taken care of that.

When Harry returned with the bottle, and poured Sophie a tankard full of Champagne, she asked him whether he was trying to raise the standards of their Brottal sundowners, which in the past had been either a cold can of Tennent's lager, or a swig of single malt whisky from a flask.

Harry sat down next to her on the bench and reached his long arm around her, pulling her in tight next to him. They clinked their tankards and watched the sun set behind the valley in front of them.

Harry kissed Sophie's forehead, and then, without any sign of nervousness or hesitation, said softly, 'Sophie Morley, will you marry me?'

Out of the pocket of his bulky green jacket, Harry pulled a little brown leather box, in which was the diamond-encrusted sapphire ring that he had had made for Sophie. It was an exact copy of the ring Sophie's father, David, had given her mother and which he'd seen from photographs at Ferryman's when he'd stayed there in the past. He had given the photographs to a friend who had become a self-taught jeweller, and he replicated it almost exactly in his studio behind Victoria Station.

Sophie recognised the ring immediately and was close to allowing her emotions get the better of her, before she composed herself. Keeping it together, just, she responded coolly,

'Are you not even going to get on one knee?'

'Do I have to? It's just that we're on a moor and that's bog we're sitting on.'

'Yes, Harry, I think you ought to,' Sophie giggled.

Harry got off the bench and onto his knee. He asked again.

'Of course I will,' Sophie smiled back at him. It was the proposal she had wanted, in a place that was incredibly special to her, by the man she knew she would spend the rest of her life with.

Sophie leant forward and kissed Harry, before throwing her arms around him tightly and resting her head against his muscular shoulder. They stayed like that for a full minute. 'Nothing could give me more pleasure in life than the thought of you being my wife,' Harry whispered into her ear.

A single tear of joy trickled down from her left eye as she kissed him again.

The sun had completely disappeared by the time they had finished their drinks, and the temperature began to plummet. They went back into the bothy to huddle by the wood burner, agreeing to tell their families that day, but waiting a few days before they let their friends know.

Sophie suggested that they took a selfie which could serve as a memory of that happy moment. By the time they took the photo, though, the light had all but disappeared, and what had meant to be a photo capturing their joy in fact looked like a strange silhouette of a couple of dark shapes. They both laughed at the prospect of their lamentable engagement photo.

*

Once they were back at the lodge, Harry told his parents their news, and another bottle of Champagne was opened. They loved Sophie like their own daughter and couldn't have been more pleased with their son's choice of wife.

With Sophie's phone finally able to pick up the WIFI from the house, she sent a message to her brother, attaching the terrible photo of their faces in darkness.

A single line of text accompanied the photograph:

Guess what, we're getting married. x

Within seconds of the message being sent, Jack called Sophie back. They had always been extremely close, and

Jack was genuinely delighted for his sister. He saw Harry as an older brother and loved nothing more than visiting the two of them in Scotland.

After speaking to his sister for a short while, during which she gave him a brief summary of the proposal and Harry's efforts to keep his knee out of the bog, he agreed to be sworn to silence until Sophie had managed to speak to her mother and Anthony first.

Putting down the phone, Harry looked in front at his computer screen, where a large logo of Brennan & Co traversed across his monitor as the screen saver.

As excited as he was to be working in a smart, professional office in the heart of London's bustling West End, deep down he knew the smoggy air and frenetic pace of a city was not for him. He would have been lying to himself if he hadn't admitted to being a tiny bit envious of the life Sophie and Harry were set to lead.

He looked across his office to see countless men all hammering away on the phones, trying to close property deals across the capital. None of them looked particularly healthy, a fact that probably wasn't helped by the two-hour lunches everyone seemed to take on a daily basis, and which were normally washed down by at least two bottles of claret. Even if Jack had decided this was how he wanted to spend the rest of his working life, he was far from certain his body would be able to manage it.

And as if compulsory work lunches were not heavy going enough, he quickly learnt that his flatmate George had made his house the de-facto after-party HQ for nights out in Fulham. It didn't help that it was positioned less than a hundred metres from Chelsea Lodge and Embargos, the local nightclubs where for at least three nights a week, energetic young men and women would ram themselves into a mirrored sweatbox of a dancefloor until 2am. Then, in the early hours, various revellers who had some tenuous claim to knowing George would begin ringing the door bell, hoping for one more drink at his infamous top-floor roof extension which he had turned into a pop-up bar, with disco balls from the ceiling and no closing time.

George had a job as a wine merchant, working for his uncle's company Harris, Winterbottom and Clarke, based in Pimlico. As his working day didn't start until 11am, calling it a night at 4am on a weeknight was manageable for him.

Within just the first week of living there, Jack was woken three times by late-night guests arriving at the house, with at least one of them walking into his room looking for a lavatory.

Jack had joined the after-party the first couple of times it happened but recognised his limitations. He was also aware that he was still on probation at Brennan & Co and had to try and give the impression at least of being a responsible and capable adult. He had resorted instead to sleeping in a pair of old ear defenders that he had in his bag, wearing an eye mask he had picked up from his recent flight back to the UK and using the lock on his bedroom door to stop random people rambling into his room at all hours.

How his life had changed from the spiritual carefreeness he had while living in Mexico only a few weeks back.

Leonardo, Diego and the others had chosen to abandon all convention and turned what was a holiday for most people into a life choice. Was that not a better option?

Thoughts of Mexico turned his mind to Lucinda and Anthony. He had forgotten that Leonardo had sent him a message yesterday saying, *Anthony seems to be getting into the swing of things*, alongside a photo of his stepfather fast asleep on the floor of the yoga deck.

He realised he had forgotten to mention this to Sophie, so decided to forward the caption of Anthony on to her, with the words:

> *Forgot to say, all seems well in paradise for our intrepid travellers. x*

Sophie had never thought her mother would have gone ahead with the holiday, even once the flights had been booked. Beaches, and certainly sleeping in yurts on beaches, had never been her thing. Sophie wondered whether she ought to have saved them by suggesting they came up to Glen Clova for the week instead, staying in one of the new cabins.

They both enjoyed being active in the outdoors, walking and watching the birds in the Highlands. Even if Jack had meant well in arranging the trip, and although she didn't say anything, Sophie feared the trip could end up causing more harm than good to her mother's already strained relationship with Anthony.

Perhaps it was a mother-daughter thing; Sophie knew Lucinda's relationship with Anthony hadn't been one of passion or love, in the way she knew she loved Harry. She had intuitively known that it was one of convenient companionship, and an understanding of mutual respect for each other's independence. Contrasting the situation to her own, she felt a wave of sadness for her mother.

She was too young to remember her father, but in her mind she maintained an image of him looking down at her, encouraging her to walk towards him when she was a young toddler. She didn't dwell on the fact that having an image of her father from this age was somewhat unrealistic, and her memory was more likely to have been formed by photographs and stories instead.

That evening, once she knew that it would by now be morning in Mexico, she called her mother and Anthony to tell them the news. They were both understandably elated, if not altogether surprised.

- Chapter Eleven -
Tulum, Mexico

Having been in Tulum for almost a full week now, Lucinda had surprised herself by how much she had actually enjoyed the trip so far. The news of Sophie's engagement only served to heighten their moods further as they approached the end of the holiday. The forthcoming wedding had certainly given her and Anthony a reliable topic of conversation, and helped break any moments of silence that arose.

Since her revelation in the rock pool earlier that week, Lucinda had come to terms with the prospect of trying to make their marriage work. She recognised that she would need to put more effort into their relationship going forward, but was also realistic, realising that it wasn't just going to turn around overnight. Assuming it could be turned around at all.

Yesterday, Anthony had arranged for them to take a private boat trip out to sea to see if they could spot some whales, having heard that a pod was recently in the vicinity and thinking it would be an interesting excursion for them to take together. Unfortunately, though, a combination of both of them getting unpleasantly seasick, and the fact that the whales had decided to head off elsewhere, meant the day didn't go quite as planned. But Lucinda did her best not to be too short with Anthony, slightly to his surprise, and they managed to laugh it off that night over a cocktail at the Camp Mayo bar.

The rest of their time had been spent walking along the beach, exploring nearby ruins and reading from the comfort of their sun beds, normally with a large glass of the flinty South Africa Sauvignon Blanc that Lucinda had become quite accustomed to over the last few days.

Having been deeply concerned by the reputation of Tulum as being a party town for her son's generation, she had been pleasantly surprised by how much she had grown to like the place. Sure, there was clearly a wild side to it if that's what you were after, but it was possible to escape from all of that too, as she and Anthony had proven.

But against all their better judgement, they had agreed for their last night, on the strong recommendation of both Leonardo and Jack, to go for dinner at Casa Jaguar.

Casa Jaguar was regarded as one of the trendiest restaurants in Tulum, set back from the main strip on the edge of the jungle. On Thursday nights, they would host their weekly jungle party, which was widely considered to be *the* place to be seen in Tulum, if you were up for a party. Reservations for dinner on Thursday evenings at Casa Jaguar usually had to be made several weeks in advance, but Leonardo was able to secure them a table. Lucinda was also persuaded by the fact that Diego would be DJing that evening, and after everything that Jack had said about him over Christmas, she thought she should at least hear him, if only for a couple of songs. Do DJs even call their music songs? she wondered to herself.

While Lucinda would never have admitted it, she was quietly anxious about her night out, partly because she hadn't been to a nightclub, and certainly not a jungle party, since she was in her early twenties. But she was also feeling nervous over the idea that she would be going on an actual date with Anthony.

On examining her outfit options that morning, Lucinda felt increasingly aware that she didn't actually have anything to wear for a smart evening in Tulum. Or anywhere, in fact, for that matter.

She couldn't remember the last time she had bought herself a proper dress; her online Boden catalogues had generally served their purpose over the years. So while Anthony was reading on the beach, Lucinda took herself off to a small boutique in the town that she had walked past a few times. It was set in what looked like a glass shipping container with minimalist style throughout. It was called simply, Daniella.

Lucinda was examining a couple of different dresses from the rail when the Argentinian shop assistant came over to help her. Lucinda had never liked the idea of a shopping assistant; if she wanted help, she would ask for it, as the last thing she wanted was a young woman monitoring her. On this occasion, however, the woman seemed so warm, with none of the peculiar grandiose presence she found women in smart clothes shops often possessed. She relaxed and allowed the woman to guide her around the store.

Soon Lucinda was in the dressing room, with a cool glass of coconut water brought to her, trying on the different styles. These were not formal cocktail dresses, but colourful linen dresses that could be worn to any occasion in the sun; from casual lunches at the pool to more formal evening parties. In the end, she went for white linen, with delicate embroidered stitching down the sides. It would certainly be appropriate for her night at Casa Jaguar and was a flattering shape for her body.

The shop assistant helped her pair it with a pair of blue and white striped espadrilles that they recommended accompanied their dresses.

It was only when she went to pay that she even thought about the price. There had been no label attached, or if there was, she hadn't noticed it. The shop assistant typed into the computer and processed a bill of 8,000 pesos. Lucinda's understanding of the exchange rate was limited, but at well over £300, she recognised this was probably multiples of what she had spent on a dress in the past. It was a lovely dress, though, and it would be tricky to walk away empty-handed now, as the young shop assistant expectantly waited for some form of payment. Out of her purse, she pulled the joint card she and Anthony used. It's as much for his benefit as it is for mine, she told herself.

That evening, she got dressed into her new clothes with a new-found level of excitement about going out.

Anthony was wearing one of his pressed navy linen shirts, where the buttons only go down halfway. Although it certainly wasn't new, it was the first time he had worn it this holiday, so it was at least clean, which Lucinda took as a sign of him trying at least a little bit.

Lucinda allowed herself a little turn in her dress, which, if there had been a mirror in the room, would have revealed it to be as flattering on her body from behind as it was from the front.

When Anthony, who had been waiting outside the yurt at their breakfast table, looked up at Lucinda as she came out ready to go, clutch bag in hand, he thought something looked different about her. Though quite what, he couldn't be totally sure. In fact, it was all new: the dress, the shoes, the bag and the youthful style.

'You look nice, Lucinda,' he uttered with sincerity, which at that moment was enough for Lucinda. She knew what he meant. They walked to the waiting taxi, hand in hand.

*

When the taxi pulled in outside the restaurant, Lucinda almost refused to get out. Her new-found confidence had abandoned her, just when she wanted it the most. It was as if all the most beautiful fashion models in the world had decided to congregate in one place for the night. What were they thinking? she thought to herself. Couldn't they have just gone to the hotel they liked before, had some tapas and a couple of drinks, and then gone back to bed for a good sleep again? All week she had slept so deeply. That's what she felt like doing, not heading out for a swanky dinner and a jungle party.

But it was too late to turn around. Anthony had already got out, paid the driver and was now standing in the short queue of about five couples waiting to be shown to their tables, as ever, apparently oblivious to his surroundings. Lucinda took a deep breath and joined him.

The restaurant had been cut into the edge of the jungle, with a courtyard built around the trees, and a large Aztec carving creating a natural divide from the bar to the restaurant area. Around the restaurant area, various replica Mayan ornaments dangled from the wooden-framed structures that had been built into the trees to form a canopy. With limited electricity available, the restaurant was lit up with hundreds of twinkling candles, and the soft glow of incense placed amongst the plants added to the decadence of the environment.

In the centre of the courtyard there were smaller tables for two and four, with the large group tables in the darker shadows on the edge of the restaurant. Although Lucinda reckoned there must have been about forty tables in total, through an imaginative use of lighting and tribal music, the restaurant was able to create an environment of intimacy.

At the back of the courtyard, a black mirrored bar had been built into a large rock face, with a circular metallic carving of some sort of shield behind it. Lucinda felt a long way from the Ostrich, her local pub in Norfolk, where the majority of her meals out had taken place over the last ten years. In fact, she couldn't remember seeing anything quite like this spectacle before, but the discretion and low lighting helped her feel more at ease.

She sat down at their table, trying to remember the last time she had been out anywhere like it. Her nerves were not helped by a square stone fountain just to her left, which had water trickling between three steps of pebbles. At the bottom of the fountain, the water was then pumped back to the top again, creating a continuous flow, which had the effect of making Lucinda feel she needed to use the lavatory.

Opposite her, Anthony was casting his eye over the cocktail list in front of him, while Lucinda marvelled at how totally at ease he was, even in these extraordinary surroundings.

The waiter brought over the two margaritas that Anthony ordered.

'Good health, darling Lucinda. What an amusing week this has been. Good old Jack,' Anthony said, raising his glass to Lucinda. One of the clever design features of the restaurant was the way in which you could still hear yourselves speak fairly easily, despite background noise from the DJ and other, often excitable, diners. It wasn't like some restaurants that Anthony had to go to with work, where he would be so focussed on having to shout over the background noise that he often ended up forgetting what it was he was going to say in the first place.

There was a pause in conversation, as there normally was when the two of them ate meals together. Lucinda finished her drink and quickly ordered two more, before

Anthony had a chance to suggest otherwise. Within seconds, two more margaritas arrived, and Anthony tried to finish his first one with the waiter somewhat awkwardly waiting by.

Lucinda decided it was time to open up to Anthony and explain her feelings with frank honesty. She knew it was a conversation that they probably should have had a long time ago, but it was with a sense of excitement and childish nervousness that she began speaking.

'Anthony, I want to be honest with you,' Lucinda said, having had a large gulp of her second margarita and breaking the silence.

'Oh yes? What about?' Anthony replied, with a face that showed no more curiosity than as if Lucinda had asked him to pass the salt.

'Over Christmas, I thought about leaving you. Starting life again. I felt our relationship had, well, you know, run its course. I felt empty. And I think you probably felt the same—'

'I did not!' Anthony interrupted, looking up briefly at Lucinda, with a face resembling a confused cocker spaniel.

The assuredness of his response slightly threw Lucinda.

'Well, that's good of you. But, listen to me, Anthony. I've been thinking a lot these last few days about everything, and I owe you an apology. Although I know we've tended to disagree about a number of things, I don't think I've been a very supportive wife to you. I want to do better. I want to reboot our relationship. You've always been nothing but decent towards me, and have given me the space I've sometimes needed. Sometimes too much space, perhaps. But I want you to know I'm grateful for that. Sometimes, though, I think perhaps I've encouraged you to give me that space. I'd like, well, maybe less space.'

Anthony was becoming evidently uncomfortable. He thought they were just going out for a fun dinner, to wrap up one of the best weeks they'd shared in a long time, and now he didn't know whether he was meant to be giving more or less space. Why are women so coded in what they say? he thought to himself. These were the sort of conversations he could not handle well.

Lucinda reached forward and put her hand on Anthony's.

'What I'm saying, darling, is that I'm sorry. I want to make this work. I am going to try harder to be closer to you, to be more supportive. I want us to be closer.'

Before Anthony had a chance to respond, their waiter returned with a large plate of local prawns and a selection of spicy dips for them. They both looked slightly confused, given they hadn't yet looked at a menu, before the waiter explained that there were no menus – just the chef's recommendations which he brought around continuously throughout the evening, and they could select whichever ones they wanted. This time, Anthony gestured for the waiter to bring another round of drinks.

He didn't really know what to say. In his mind, he was aware they hadn't been particularly close in recent years, and that there had been almost no sexual contact between them for ages. But none of that had really bothered him. In fact, he'd actually been more than fine with that arrangement. He remained enormously fond of Lucinda, and just knowing she was around, pottering in the house, was more than sufficient for him. He liked the way they tottered on in their own gentle way. He wasn't really sure why Lucinda suddenly felt she wanted to change things. Everything had been working rather well, he thought.

But then he digested again the reality of what Lucinda had initially said; that she had been preparing to leave him. *Leave me!* he thought, after everything he had done for her over the years. After educating her children, who he had quickly come to think of as his own; after paying off the mortgage on their house; providing her with a generous income each year and after giving everything he had to her. Having been loyal, and steady, and true, throughout all of her emotional ups and downs. The fact the woman he thought he knew so well could be quite so flippant about their marriage surprised him. Part of him felt a little hurt, possibly even angry for a moment. But looking up across the table at Lucinda, in her new dress and with her huge green eyes, he realised he didn't have it in him to be angry with her, for deep down he knew he loved her. And this was perhaps her strange way of dealing with things.

In the end, all Anthony could muster was, 'Well, Lucinda, I'm very pleased to hear you've come to that conclusion. I'm not sure I would know what to do without you, to be honest.'

'You won't have to, Anthony. I'm right here, and I think we've got a lot to look forward to ahead of us, together.'

He wanted to change the subject, and when the waiter returned with their next dish, the baby fish taco selection, he went for a line of just how much he had enjoyed the

Mexican food that week: 'Do you think tacos would taste as good with partridge in them? Could be a fun new dish to serve.'

*

As soon as Lucinda had opened up to him, she felt lighter, as if a large weight had been lifted from her shoulders. Even though she expected it to have little impact on him, she felt better with herself for being honest about the situation with him. And she really was going to try to make this work, she told herself.

After another round of margaritas and several dishes of chef specials later, they felt as if they were as young as everyone else in the restaurant and in the early days of their relationship. Lucinda looked at her watch and saw that it was almost midnight. The music had subtly increased in volume and tempo over the course of the evening, and from behind the courtyard, they could see that a whole new area of the restaurant was opening up further into the jungle, where the party had evidently started.

'What do you think? Should we call it a night and head back now?' Anthony asked, after paying the dinner bill. His head was starting to feel a bit heavy; neither of them had drunk nearly that much tequila since they were students.

Lucinda had enjoyed the evening enormously, but she was also feeling like she had drunk too much and wanted little more now than to curl up next to Anthony, back in the comfort of their yurt. She nodded, with a little shrug of her nose, which Anthony knew meant, *Let's give this a miss and get out of here.*

He asked the waiter, who was just printing off Anthony's receipt from the card machine, if he could arrange a taxi for them.

'C'mon, sir, you have to go to the party for one drink at least. This is Casa Jaguar, on a Thursday! You must experience the energy of the jungle, at least for a short while,' the waiter said, smiling to them both.

Anthony looked to Lucinda for a sign, who shrugged her shoulders. That wasn't exactly a definitive no; and if Anthony told the waiter they were still leaving, he'd think Anthony was pulling his wife home from the party.

'Fine. We'll go for one drink then,' Anthony said, patting the table with his left hand in a moment of uncharacteristic enthusiasm.

Lucinda raised her eyebrows and smiled while shaking her head, not in disapproval, but finding herself surprised at the situation they found themselves in.

Their waiter, who seemed as pissed as the rest of the restaurant, gave them both a high five, before pulling out two shot glasses from his black pouch in front of him and a bottle of what looked like tequila that he had attached to his belt. At the bottom of the bottle, Anthony could see a large worm, and gold flakes floating around. It seemed that he'd been going around the tables and consuming as many of the shots as he distributed.

'Oh Lordy! No, I couldn't possibly have one of those,' Anthony protested, but the waiter had already filled both of their shot glasses to the brim. He then pulled out a third glass, which he also filled to the brim, and showed them how it was done.

'We do these together, because tonight, we are all a united family in the jungle.' At that, the waiter threw the shot down his neck. Anthony and Lucinda followed his instructions and immediately felt their throats erupt in fiery pain.

'What on earth was that?' Lucinda spluttered at the waiter, her eyes watering.

'It's my magic *mezcal*. You'll like it. Enjoy your evening, guys.'

'I bloody don't like it,' Lucinda replied, still holding her throat.

Anthony raised his hand to wave the waiter off; it seemed easier at that particular moment, he thought, than trying to talk.

A few moments later, the fire in their throats soothed, Anthony said, 'Right, let's go and have one drink, and then head home, shall we?'

Lucinda grabbed Anthony's hand and they headed around the side of the courtyard, behind which was a hidden garden with a DJ booth set up under a stone archway at the far end. It was Diego, and the 400-strong crowd were loving him. Everywhere they looked, spacey-eyed people were rocking their bodies to the beat of the bass. They considered leaving again, thinking they had seen enough, but had agreed to have a final drink. On the other side of the garden, deeper into the jungle, there were a couple of tables. Parked on the bench, Anthony suggested she stay there and keep the table while he tackled the crowd at the bar.

'What would you like?' he asked.

'Certainly nothing with tequila or the magic mezcal. A glass of white wine, I think. Anything to wash out the taste in my mouth!' Lucinda shouted back, into his ear.

Lucinda watched Anthony make his way through the crowd until he was lost amongst them. Their table had rather protected them from where the crowd were jostling for central position, though allowed Lucinda a clear view to where Diego was spinning his decks. With a cigarette in one hand and a bottle of beer in the other, even Lucinda could see how captivating Diego was. How extraordinary, she thought to herself, that she was at a jungle party in Mexico that her 23-year-old son had been at only a few weeks earlier. Although Diego's music wasn't exactly what she was normally accustomed to, she could see why he was so popular. There was something hypnotic about it. Lucinda couldn't help but find herself rocking her head to the music in an appreciative way, along with the crowd in front of her.

Lucinda looked up at the sky, where the stars were glittering brightly above the darkness of the jungle, and for the first time in a long time she felt genuinely happy and free from a sense of burden. She knew that she should stop trying to look for something that wasn't there, but instead make what was there – her friends, her children and her kind, decent husband – the best they could be. She just needed to navigate that path of life with consideration and thoughtfulness and add a little more adventure.

Her thoughts were rather swiftly interrupted by the voice of a young American man, wearing a maroon t-shirt which accentuated his muscular arms and chest. The man was with three other friends, each of whom was as equally athletic as the first.

'May we squeeze in here, ma'am?' asked the man, smiling at Lucinda. He couldn't be much older than Jack, Lucinda thought to herself.

Given the table had two benches on either side which could easily sit six on each, it was difficult for Lucinda to do anything but agree.

'Yes, of course. My husband's just gone to the bar to get drinks, but please do squeeze in.'

'You have a lovely accent, ma'am. And that is a beautiful dress,' the man said, smiling in a way that reminded Lucinda of a puppy wanting to please its master. Well intentioned, but not what was asked for.

'That's very kind of you, thank you,' she replied. Before adding, a little awkwardly, 'Are you guys on holiday here?' As if they could be on any other sort of trip.

'We are, ma'am. We've just come back from Afghanistan and we're now on our R&R.'

Good heavens, Lucinda thought, soldiers. But they didn't look old enough to be in Afghanistan. 'Please. You're very polite, but do stop calling me "ma'am". I'm Lucinda. Now what do you mean by "R&R"?'

The man smiled to his friends with a knowing grin, and then responded. 'Rest and Recuperation, Lucinda.'

'Of course, how silly of me. Sorry. And what's your name?'

'I'm Sean. Sean J. Cooper. I'm from San Diego.'

'And how long have you been a soldier for, Sean J. Cooper?' *Christ, am I flirting with him?* Lucinda thought to herself. *I'm probably older than his mother.*

'I'm not a soldier, ma'am. Sorry, Lucinda.'

'You're not?'

'No, I'm a Seal.'

Lucinda thought now it was all a joke and he was just teasing her, before he added, 'I'm a Navy Seal,' looking at her for recognition.

Lucinda's knowledge of US military was limited, but by chance she had read an interview recently in the weekend supplement of *The Times* about a Navy Seal called Robert O'Neill who had written a book claiming to be the one who shot Osama bin Laden, during their late-night raid in the Pakistani compound, the account of which was now being called into question by some of his comrades. What was not in question, however, was that the Navy Seals were considered to be the toughest of the US military, rather like the British Special Forces.

Lucinda knew the sensible thing to do at this point would have been to make her excuses and go to find Anthony at the bar. But she didn't. Instead, she said, 'Oh, so you're one of the tough guys, are you, the ones who shot Bin Laden?'

Sean J. Cooper smiled and looked back to his friends again, who seemed to be encouraging him to continue their conversation. 'Lucinda, Seals don't talk about who they shoot and don't shoot. It's against our code. But we've all seen some pretty bushy places.'

'I'm sure, and that must be why you're here then. Coming back to the real world?'

'I don't mind if the things I see here are bushy or totally shaven, I'm just here to have a good time.'

There was a cackle of laughter from the other men. Lucinda realised what Sean J. Cooper was referring to.

'That is no way to speak in front of a woman old enough to be your mother, Sean J. Cooper. My husband would be very cross,' retorted Lucinda, but whether it was the tequila or the madness of the whole situation, she allowed the conversation to continue.

'Well, I'm sorry, Lucinda. Listen, please do have a drink with us so I can make amends. Just one?'

'My husband's literally just gone to get me a drink. He'll be back soon.'

'I'm sure. But here, have one of our Coronas in the meantime.' Sean leant across to the bucket of beers that his friend was holding and passed Lucinda an open Corona.

*

The tables in the courtyard where Anthony and Lucinda had been having supper had rapidly been cleared and now a scrum of party-goers were jostling to order drinks from the bar, which was now fully manned and distributing cocktails at an impressive rate.

Anthony was making his way to join the back of the queue when to his left a Mexican man of about thirty, wearing a blue t-shirt and holding his backpack, caught his eye. The man spoke to him, but Anthony wasn't able to hear properly, so joined him, explaining, 'Sorry, what did you say? My head's pounding, and I can't hear a thing with this music!'

His response, Anthony thought, was along the lines of, 'Would you like a pill? It's good for your head, yes?'

That's thoughtful of him, Anthony thought. When he was younger, he would always take a couple of paracetamols before going to bed after a night out, and found that it did wonders for his head the following morning. This man must think along the same lines.

'Great idea, that's very kind of you,' Anthony said. 'You'd better give me two, I think.'

'Ha! Be careful, you crazy man,' the man replied, before reaching into his bag.

Anthony wasn't quite sure why he called him a crazy man, and worried he was probably coming across drunker than he realised. He took the pills from the man and swallowed them both in one. The man offered him some water, which Anthony was grateful for, as the second pill had got slightly lodged in his throat.

'You're very kind, you're very kind. Can I buy you a drink?' Anthony asked.

'No, mister, just give me the *pesos* please. 300 *pesos*,' the man replied, abruptly.

'Yes, sure, of course,' Anthony said, and pulled out 300 *pesos* from his wallet and handed them to the man.

The man nodded and wished him a good night.

Strange encounter, Anthony thought to himself, and somewhat rude of the man, but he thought no more of it and joined the back of the queue. Ten minutes later, he'd reached the bar, squeezing himself between two American guys requesting a bucket full of Coronas and a bottle of tequila.

'A glass of wine and bottle of Corona, please,' Anthony said, before then looking back at the queue behind him and adding, 'sorry, please double that. Two wines and two Coronas, in a bucket, please!'

'We don't normally serve wine by the glass in a bucket, sir. But we can give you a tray if you like,' the waiter responded.

'Oh, go on, mister, just this once. Give old Uncle Anthony here a bucket, please. I do like the buckets, so very much.' The man looked at Anthony oddly, yet with a knowing smile. In some part of his brain, Anthony was aware of what he had just said, but yet had no recognition of why. Definitely overdid the booze, he thought, but was pleasantly surprised that he felt more energised than he could remember in a long while.

'Okay, Uncle Anthony, just this once.' The barman winked at him, handing him a bucket with his drinks.

Smiling, Anthony turned back from the bar and made his way through the crowd, while shouting, 'Mind out! Mind out! Uncle Anthony coming through, with an unexpected bucket.'

Once back in the courtyard, he saw there was a path around the other side of the bar which led back around to the secret garden. It looked like an interesting alternative route, he thought. *He comes from one way, but he shall go back another way*, he said to himself.

He picked one of the bottles of Corona out of the bucket and took a big glug. He couldn't remember a beer tasting as good as this before, ever.

'Wow, this tastes amazing,' he told a couple leaning

against the structure behind him. They laughed and told him they were pleased to hear that.

Again, somewhere inside his head, he was trying to establish why it was he felt so good. He looked ahead and could only see a sea of bodies to get through. What was even down that way? he wondered. Was it the same garden he had come from, or was this a different garden? He closed his eyes for a moment to listen to the music, and could feel the bass enter his body through the soles of his feet. It travelled through him, forcing his knees to instantly shift to the dance. Then to his hips. They needed to move.

Then the beat got higher, into his arms, which wanted to rise into the air together. He could hear a voice saying, *Don't keep this beat to yourself. Share it. Share it with all those around you.* He put down the bucket by his feet and opened his palms. Through his fingers, he released the beat into the crowd of people in front of him. He opened his eyes and watched proudly as those in the crowd ahead of him passed the beat around. He could see it. He could see their bodies moving as the beat passed through their bodies too, and he was proud. He was proud he had shared it.

He took another swig of his Corona and leant back on the wall behind him, watching the people dancing in the crowd in front of him, and moving his head along to the rhythm of Diego's music. He was about to raise his hands into the air again, when he felt a tap on his shoulder. At first, he thought someone had just brushed against him. But then it came again, more assertively. He turned around. There, standing in front of him, smiling, and wearing a pair of leopard print trousers and a buttoned-up velvet black jacket with just a bra underneath was the woman from Camp Mayo.

'The yoga's obviously been good for you,' the woman smiled.

- Chapter Twelve -
Tulum, Mexico

Anthony stared at the woman standing in front of him, slightly lost for words. He thought for a moment that he might be having a flashback. Before he could think of anything to say, the woman asked, 'Is one of those for me?' Looking towards the bucket Anthony was clasping containing two glasses of wine and the second bottle of Corona.

'Yes! Yes, absolutely. I bought both options – beer and wine – just in case I bumped into you as I wasn't sure what you like to drink.'

'Well, I'm afraid you're wrong on both counts. I take scotch and soda, but I'll have one of these wines then, if that's okay.'

'Absolutely, have both of them if you want,' Anthony hastily replied.

'Perhaps I'll start with one and see how we do, shall I?' the woman said, smiling.

'Good idea,' and with that, Anthony passed her the wine.

'I didn't expect to see you here. Didn't have it down as your sort of place. Then again, I guess there are a lot of misconceptions about people out here. Or maybe we pretend to be things we're not. Anyway, you look like you're having a good evening?'

'Not really. Well, I wasn't having one earlier. In fact, my wife of twenty-two years told me she was planning to leave me. Not very nice at all, given everything I've done for her. In fact, that bloody woman has got some nerve.'

'Sorry, you said your wife? You have a wife? And she's here too, with you?' the woman in green said, clearly a little surprised.

'Yep. She's around here somewhere. God, I'm so sorry. I really shouldn't be saying things like this. But, honestly, how could she have said something like that? Who treats a spouse quite so… flippantly?'

'I'm sorry to hear that; she sounds like a bitch. And I have to say, I'm kinda surprised to hear you're here with a wife at all.'

Anthony looked slightly offended and the woman explained.

'It's just that each time I've seen you, you've been alone. I kind of assumed you were here by yourself. So, has she left you now?'

'I honestly don't know. She says she is, then she isn't, then she is. Who knows, you mystery lady, who knows!' Anthony wiggled his finger towards the woman in a way he thought was amusing, to emphasise the curiosity of the situation.

'Right…' she answered in a drawn-out way. 'Maybe you should go and find her?'

'No. Do you know what? No! I've given everything to that woman, and she repays me by saying she's going to leave me. Anyway, what about you? You here on your own?' he slurred.

'I am now. I travelled here with some friends, but they've gone back to Chicago. After I got offered a few extra days by the hotel, I thought I'd stay on and enjoy it a while longer. I leave tomorrow afternoon, actually.'

Anthony had a flashback. 'Oh my God. I'm so sorry about the situation on the toilet the other evening. That was so embarrassing.'

'Embarrassing? Why? You didn't know I was there.'

'Of course I didn't, but you know, I think I saw your, well, I think I saw your breasts,' he blurted out, finding it hard to believe what had just come out of his mouth a split second later.

'You did, did you? I wondered.' The woman raised her left eyebrow knowingly.

'Can I tell you something?'

'Of course.'

'I haven't been able to get the thought of your nipples out of my head ever since that moment. I almost thought, well, I almost thought you *wanted* me to see them.'

'What would you do if I told you I did? It's not often a woman, on holiday by themselves, finds a handsome man looking at their tits in such an enthusiastic, yet gentlemanly way, late at night.'

Anthony felt a rush of blood charge around his body. He was suddenly aroused in a way he hadn't felt for as long as he could remember. And, in fact, just generally, though he couldn't understand why, he felt more alive than he could ever remember feeling. He darted his eyes down to the woman's partially exposed breasts again, which she saw.

'Did you like what you saw? You're a very handsome man, Mr...?'

'Anthony. I'm Anthony,' he answered before grabbing the second Corona from his bucket and taking a large swig. 'Yes, Ms Americano, you can call me Anthony.'

'Would you like to walk me back to our camp? It's a lovely walk back along the beach, under the stars.'

*

Back at the military table, Lucinda was now deep in conversation with Sean and his friends, who had joined in. She had allowed herself to be distracted from Anthony's whereabouts, assuming he'd been held up at the bar and was too polite to push through the crowd. Sean's friends were telling her stories about their time together in the Seals. Not the sort of tales of war bravado you might expect from some soldiers, but about the bonds they'd formed and the camaraderie they'd developed working together over the last few years.

In the background, Diego's music had become more upbeat, with a stronger Mexican influence to it than before. People started dancing more intimately.

'Lucinda, how about we dance? Just until your husband comes back?' Sean asked.

'Um, I'm not sure, actually. I don't really dance, but thank you anyway,' she replied hesitantly, a little embarrassed at the proposal.

His friends then all jumped in, 'Oh go on, give our man a dance, Mrs Robinson.'

'Just one?' he pleaded with her.

'Fine. Okay, just one,' wondering what on earth Anthony would think if he arrived back to see her on the dance floor with a young American soldier.

Sean stood up, taking Lucinda by the hand, and led her slightly away from the table. Diego was playing a remixed version of a song Lucinda recognised from when Jack had been playing it during Christmas, called *Despacito*.

She put her head back and allowed him to direct her hips.

'You can dance, girl. You can dance!' Sean hollered towards her. And Lucinda could dance. She'd been resolutely avoiding dance floors for so long now that she'd forgotten how much she enjoyed it.

Sean put his left hand through her hair and lowered it slowly down the side of her body, before resting it hovering over her right buttock. The song drew out, and over the mic, Diego thanked the crowd before announcing he was taking a short ten-minute break.

Lucinda felt the alcohol wearing off and suddenly felt enormously tired.

'You know, Sean, it was great to meet you and your friends, but I've got to go and find my husband and go to bed. I'm exhausted.'

'Won't you stay, just for a while longer?'

'No, I really must go. But you guys enjoy your night.'

'What about one quick kiss, Lucinda? I'd so love to kiss you.'

'Don't be so ridiculous! You've clearly been in the desert far too long. Go and find someone your own age.'

Lucinda gave Sean a hug and, feeling quite proud of herself and flattered by the attention she had been given, headed towards the bar to find Anthony.

*

Anthony and Ms Americano by this point had finished their bucket of drinks and had taken another two tequila shots from the passing waitresses wearing gunslinger belts loaded with shot glasses. Having also danced to *Despacito*, they had found a swinging seat behind the edge of the garden, on an entrance path to the jungle.

By now, the two pills and tequila were having a full impact, and the endorphins were charging around Anthony's body. Everyone and everything he looked at gave him enormous pleasure. He lay back on the swinging hammock and put his arm around the Ms Americano. She smiled and lay back with him, resting her head upon his shoulder.

'Do you know what's strange?' Anthony said, with his head towards the woman.

'What's that?' she replied.

'That I don't even know you. At all, in fact. I literally know nothing about your life. And yet, I think – I *know* even – I love you. I just want you to be so happy.'

'You're ridiculous. A completely mad Englishman,' she laughed at Anthony.

'Would you like to go for a walk? Somewhere more private?' Anthony said, surprising even himself with his new-found confidence.

'You have a wife! And she's here, at this party! Have you gone completely mad?' she answered, still giggling.

'I have a wife who earlier this evening told me she was planning on leaving me. I have a wife who for 99% of our marriage has not shown me the blindest bit of attention. I have a wife who I have not had sex with for about ten years. I have a wife who has been in love with another man for the duration of our marriage!' Anthony looked up to the burning bright stars above him, and with his drink toasted his wife's late husband: 'Yup, thanks, David.'

'Who's David?'

'The man my wife is in love with.'

'Oh wow. She's having an affair?'

'Fortunately not. He lives up there. He's dead.'

'I see.'

Anthony continued to stare up at the stars in contemplation. The woman leaned over and kissed him. He kissed her back, feeling her soft lips against his.

'Okay. Let's get out of here,' the woman whispered.

*

Lucinda did what she thought was two full circuits of the bar in her search for Anthony. After the first one, she embarrassed herself by bumping straight back into the young soldiers. She couldn't face seeing them again on the second loop, so she turned back towards the restaurant area. There were now too many people to move, and even if she was close to Anthony, which she expected she was, she would have had to almost walk straight into him in order to find him. The music had become even louder, and Lucinda was unable to see above the heads of anyone else around.

This is getting silly, she thought to herself. *What on earth are we doing at this party anyway? We'll never find each other here.* If Anthony was wandering around looking for her, Lucinda assumed he would soon enough have the same thought – to head back to the camp. She turned back past the reception and headed to the exit.

If she had looked behind on her way out, she would have seen Anthony and the woman in green emerging from the back garden. Fortunately for Anthony, she did not.

As she walked through the doorway, a hostess in a little black dress and holding a clipboard was standing in front of the entrance, restricting people coming in and out. To Lucinda's surprise, she saw a queue of people trailing about three hundred metres down the road, all trying to get into the jungle party. Why people spent their entire evening queueing, and instead didn't just go and start another party elsewhere, she had no idea.

The hostess waved at one of the official taxis from the rank opposite the entrance, and thanked Lucinda for coming. The driver opened the door and drove Lucinda the 1.5km back to Camp Mayo. The night security man was standing by the gate of the camp, shined a torchlight towards the path in front of her and escorted her back to their yurt.

Lucinda wondered whether she would find Anthony asleep already in their bed, having given up looking for her much earlier in the evening. To her surprise, he wasn't there, but moments later she had tucked herself in the sheets, resting her tequila-swollen head against the pillow, without any concern for his whereabouts. She was convinced that he would make his own way back shortly and she'd wake up to find him lying next to her. They were flying home tomorrow and the last thing she wanted was a throbbing head for the journey. She drifted off to sleep.

*

The woman in the little black dress asked Anthony whether they needed a taxi as they left, as she had done only moments earlier, of Lucinda.

'It's okay, thanks. We're going to walk,' the woman in green answered, before Anthony had a chance to say anything.

'Well, have a good night then, guys.'

They crossed the road and walked past the now closed beach bar opposite, and onto the sandy beach behind. The woman pointed out a small campfire burning about two miles down the beach.

'That's our camp. Do you think you'll be okay to walk that?' the woman asked.

'Of course I will. I wish it was further. I can't remember the last time I felt this happy.'

The water from the breaking waves was just touching the edge of their feet. In the background, the sound of the jungle party could still be heard about the rustle of palm trees around them. Anthony felt he'd become an extension of the environment around him, like an additional palm tree, only slightly more mobile and human.

The light of the burning campfire in the distance was becoming clearer. A warm breeze blew gently on their backs, carrying the now muffled beat of the jungle party towards them, as if beckoning them back. Anthony began explaining how this held deep meaning; an analogy of how mankind can never truly leave the grip of the jungle, regardless of how developed and sophisticated it became.

Before he had a chance to effectively explain this metaphor to the woman, she slid her hand into his and was now leading him up off the main stretch of the beach and into the dunes behind them.

Behind the first dune there was a patch of wavy grass. They sat down, and after only a short moment the woman wrapped her legs around Anthony, pushing him back onto the sand. He looked up at the stars above again before closing his eyes and resting his head against the sand.

With his right hand, he picked up a handful of the cold Mexican sand and let it seep through his open fingers, appreciating the texture of each single grain and trying to let himself believe this was truly happening. With his left hand, he stroked the woman's back, disregarding the sound of distant voices from others on the beach.

He felt his belt buckle being opened, and the top button of his chinos was soon undone. The woman then pulled his trousers down, past his ankles, removing his blue check boxer shorts at the same time.

When Anthony re-opened his eyes he couldn't bring himself to avert his gaze from the sky to see what was happening, when he felt a petite hand clasp his rapidly swelling cock, while another slowly massaged his much-neglected balls. Any concerns he'd had over the ability to use his cock after such a long period of abstinence were banished. There was life in the old fella yet, he thought to himself.

The hand on his balls was then replaced by a tongue, which slowly worked its way up along the base of his cock. Circulating the tip of her tongue around every part of his shaft, she then wrapped her lips around his head and allowed the top half of his cock into her warm throat. Now on her knees in front of him, she moved her head back and forth, up and down, while her tongue continued to circulate around the head of his cock.

After a few minutes of this, she pulled her head back and tied her hair back. At some point in the process, she had removed her underwear, and now straddled herself above Anthony's plentiful cock. With her left hand, she grasped his sturdy shaft and directed it inside her, before slowly allowing gravity to do its job.

With the support of her left hand, she drove herself against Anthony repeatedly. At sixty years of age, she had become accustomed to knowing what she wanted, and going about getting it in the way she wanted. Anthony was only too happy to oblige. Her moans became louder with each repetition and he could feel her juices running down onto him. She lowered her now bare chest down so her erect nipples hovered on the edge of Anthony's lips, close enough for him to suck.

After several minutes that Anthony hoped would never end, the woman moved her tongue into Anthony's mouth before whispering, 'Come with me.' He did so, almost on demand, filling the woman with what felt like a lost decade.

They took a deep inhale as they tried to catch their breath. On opening their eyes, they both noticed what seemed like a spotlight from a torch shine past them. The woman slid herself off Anthony, and as she did so, he noticed for the first time a tattoo of a shooting star on her inner thigh, just to the left of her vagina.

- Chapter Thirteen -

London, UK

The offices of Brennan & Co were within a large modern glass building off Baker Street. It seemed to be a popular place for property companies, with Knight Frank headquarters around the corner and CBRE opposite them.

Jack would cycle into the office in the morning, up the Fulham Road, until he reached South Kensington, at which point he would cut up Exhibition Road and into Hyde Park. From there he could cut past the memorial fountain for Princess Diana, over the Serpentine Bridge, and straight up the cycle path to Marble Arch, normally catching the Household Cavalry returning to Knightsbridge Barracks from their morning exercise ride out.

By the time he reached his office, it was about 7.30am, which normally gave him at least half an hour to have a shower, get changed, and begin reading the emails that came into the team overnight before his boss, Angus, arrived shortly after 8am.

Even though he knew he didn't want to work in property for the rest of his life, he had enjoyed much of his first few weeks at the company, and felt he had been positioned in a good department dealing with the private client side of the business. His first project was to try and find a buyer for an office block behind Carnaby Street, a property that one of their South African clients recently mentioned in passing that he owned, and could do with shifting. Then he had a Turkish man on his books who was after both a house and an office, ideally combined. The eclectic mixture of clients kept it interesting.

When he was at his desk, he tried to avoid using his phone as much as possible, choosing instead to clear groups of WhatsApp messages that came through during his lunch break. But this morning, when he saw an alert come through from the "Tulum Tigers", he picked his phone up and opened the message. It was from Kyle, an American guy who worked at the Papaya Playa beach bar, and also understudied Diego sometimes as a DJ.

Walking back last night along the strip with a couple of guys from work... decide to cut across to the beach for the final stretch, and then came across this... Look familiar, Jack?

Jack pushed the download button on his phone, to find a naked Noelle riding another man in the sand.

Jack laughed and responded to the group:

Yup, thanks for that! I'd tried to put that out of my mind. Glad to see she's still got it, though.

A couple of moments later, Jack left his desk and went to the bathroom. He opened up the video and played it again. There was no doubt it was Noelle, but it was the man in the video, with his cream chinos rolled down to his ankles, that he was more interested in. He zoomed in closer and ran the video in slow time, conscious that if anyone walked in, they would think he was some kind of sick pervert. For much of the video the man had his head buried in Noelle's tits, but towards the end, *clearly when the man is climaxing,* Jack thought with a shudder, he moves back and collapses against the sand. Jack zoomed in on this part as much as his trusty iPhone 6 with a shattered screen allowed. The face looked uncomfortably familiar.

Surely not, he told himself. He looked again. There, romping with his own holiday fling from a few weeks earlier, was his stepfather, Anthony. It was even in almost the exact same spot behind the beach.

Sickened, he put his phone away and took the stairs down to the ground floor exit of the building. He walked out onto Baker Street, on a cold and cloudy January morning, and took himself for a walk towards Portman Square. He continued left onto Wigmore Street, and up towards Cavendish Square Gardens where he found a bench to sit on. He pulled out his phone and watched the video again, torturing himself with the horror of the situation, and felt an overwhelming concern for his mother.

He was staggered that Anthony, of all people, could have betrayed his mother like that, though he knew deep down that she could be dismissive and unpleasant towards him. Despite that, Jack had never had him down as a philandering zipper, like so many middle-aged men he had come across.

Another part of him felt angry and slightly disturbed at seeing Noelle, whose vagina he had spent forty minutes intimately massaging as part of Leonardo's mad *yoni* massaging classes, before he spent at least that again fucking her in the dunes as roughly as she had requested. Despite her being older than his mother, he felt at least some sort of bond had been struck between them. And now she was fucking someone else, so quickly, in the very same spot. And not any old person. His bloody stepfather! The man who had brought him up. This was beyond weird. What would happen now? What was he meant to do? He started to feel physically sick.

He looked at the names on the WhatsApp group. It was only Leonardo who could possibly recognise the man in the video and make the connection, but he was unlikely to look too closely and recognise him through the blur.

He thought about calling his sister, but suspected she would take an emotional and likely irrational approach to the whole situation. Besides, he didn't want her to have to come down from her post-engagement high. There was also the risk that she would probably blame him for sending them on the trip in the first place.

What the fuck am I meant to do now?, he said to himself. Beyond the immediate problem that his stepfather was having sex with a woman behind his mother's back, he was also concerned that the video could end up going viral on the internet.

While he was equally guilty of having forwarded similar videos he had been sent on his phone to other groups on a number of occasions, he understandably wanted to stop this one in its tracks. It wasn't just because of the potential humiliation due to Anthony's participation; he also wanted to protect Noelle, and what was left of her dignity. He hardly knew her but, despite her age and naughty antics, he knew there was a vulnerability about her, which is what had led her to Tulum in the first place.

He decided to call Kyle, and asked him to promise to delete the video and withdraw it from the group. To his comfort, Kyle understood and agreed. He immediately deleted it from the group chat, but only after Jack had already saved his own copy of the film. Only one other person in the group had responded, and the others were most likely still asleep.

In the end, Jack decided that the best course of action was, in fact, not to do anything immediately. He would wait and see how the situation panned out first.

He could still send a text to his mother, he thought, just to check in. Although WhatsApp was a technological step too far for her, she was a prolific texter.

Everything going okay out there? All set for your trip home? J x

He thought that her response would be a good indicator of what to expect. He looked at his watch and knew it would be nearly 7am there now, and she would soon be awake if she wasn't already.

He stood up from his bench and began walking back towards the office. A few minutes later, he heard his phone ping. Lucinda had replied.

Had a surprisingly glorious time, actually. Even went to your jungle party last night and managed to completely lose your stepfather. We both seem to have made it home in the end, though! Thank you, darling. Love, your mother x

His mother clearly didn't know anything yet. Jack felt the only thing he could do was to allow things, at least initially, to play themselves out. They actually went to the jungle party, which was unexpected in itself. Something bonkers must have happened there, he thought to himself.

As he sat at his desk for the rest of the day, he was in a state of perpetual confusion, wondering just what exactly had led to this all happening, and questioning his own responsibility in the sordid situation.

Even though he knew his mother wasn't particularly loving to Anthony, thanks to his congenial manner, he had always assumed that he was okay with that. He'd always been so fond of Anthony. His stepfather had been nothing but decent, not just to Lucinda, but to Sophie and Jack too, for the whole of his living memory. He just wasn't the sort to mess around behind his mother's back. It was just not his style. With a melting pot of conflicting emotions and loyalties, Jack found himself in unchartered territory.

He swung from a natural protectiveness over his mother, to a reasoned understanding towards his stepfather for wanting to break the sexual dormancy he had grown to live with.

But the woman who had brought sex back into Anthony's life was the same woman he had romped with only a few weeks earlier. Was there an element of jealousy or competition that he felt towards Anthony? He found himself stuck in some strange incestuous love triangle with the man he'd grown up with as his father, and there was no one he could talk to about it. No one in the world who'd fully understand.

He left work at 5pm on the dot, without saying goodbye to his colleagues. He decided to leave his bicycle locked in its place in the basement, and instead walk back to the flat in Fulham, hoping the icy January air would help clear his head as he tried to make some sense of the totally fucked-up situation. Every now and again along the walk, he pulled out his phone and watched the shameful video again, where Noelle rode his stepfather in the same ferocious manner he had experienced a few weeks earlier. Utterly appalled, he tried to ignore the fact that he was also slightly turned on by seeing her again.

By the time he reached Stamford Bridge on the Fulham Road, where Chelsea became Fulham, his head was still in turmoil and the last thing he felt like doing was spending the evening with George, his flatmate. Instead, he turned back on himself and walked the 200 yards back down the Fulham Road until he reached the corner of the Billings, a small mews street that had a little pub, The Pensioner, tucked away at the end of the road. Unlike most the pubs nearby that now called themselves gastropubs, The Pensioner had steadfastly refused to change. The only food it sold was pork scratchings and crisps. It was a good old-fashioned boozer.

Jack sat himself down quietly in the far corner and started drinking.

- Chapter Fourteen -

La Touche Vineyard, Franschhoek, South Africa

Lucinda found the notion of autumn approaching peculiar. She had been in the Franschhoek Valley in the Western Cape for nearly three weeks now, and it had been nothing but glorious sunshine. Admittedly, the temperature had started to drop a little in the evenings, but it was nothing compared to the dreary autumns that she was used to.

She was loving her time on the wine farm, with her cousin Pauline. Their working day would start at 11am, when the tasting rooms would open, and there would normally be a small queue of visitors waiting to get in by the time she unlocked the door. She and Pauline would run the tastings, while Greg, Pauline's husband, ran the winemaking side of the operation.

The whole set-up had been far more professionally run and much more slick than she had been led to believe from her various emails with her cousin over the years. She hadn't even glanced at the vineyard's website, and so was rather blown away on arrival. She had visited only once before when the children were young, and had remembered only a slightly run-down farm that felt more like a family home. It had most certainly been spruced up now.

The rapid improvements in the vineyard all started, Pauline had told her, when a wealthy French banking family bought the vineyard down the road, Simondium, and visitors' expectations shot up quickly for all of the vineyards in the vicinity. They had to up their game, or otherwise faced losing out. Although Pauline and Greg did miss the more relaxed approach they used to have in the valley, from a business perspective, all the vineyards were doing better than they had ever done before. Not just from increased sales and global awareness of the quality of South African wine, but because of the sheer number of visitors coming wine tasting and for lunch each day. Some even brought a picnic to eat amongst their vines, which was permitted if not encouraged.

Lucinda enjoyed meeting the far-flung visitors from all over the world, some from places she had never even heard of. What she found quite peculiar was how many visitors didn't actually drink. They catered for these guests by offering a selection of olive oils to taste, as well as fruit cordials, and more often than not, they bought a bottle of wine as a guest too.

At 5pm, the last visitors would leave, the security gates would close, and Pauline and Lucinda would often open one of the better bottles which they kept separately, and which would never normally be offered for tasting.

Pauline and Greg were particularly fortunate with the positioning of their vineyard, set high up on the west side of the hill overlooking the valley, so they had sun much later than most of the other vineyards nearby, with the most wonderful sunsets. The evening light fell onto the magnificent mountains in front of them, rising with such power and in stark contrast to the sleepy civility of the Franschhoek village below.

On this particular Friday evening, as it was coming to the end of the month, Pauline had to run through the wine sale numbers with the accountant, so she waited in the tasting rooms and told Lucinda she would catch up with her later.

Lucinda took a twelve-year-old bottle of Pinotage, their signature wine, from the private collection they kept and headed up to her favourite spot, a bench on the edge of the reservoir, right at the top of the vineyard.

Every time Lucinda sat on the bench and looked out across the valley, she felt a rush of appreciation for life and the majesty of it all in front of her. How lucky she was to be able to have this view all to herself. That evening, Lucinda noticed that the particular angle of the light, reflecting off the bald rock face high up on the mountain, made the view even more beautiful than normal.

She had had time to do a lot of thinking since that fateful morning in Mexico at the end of their holiday three months ago, when Anthony woke up, and recounted the details of his evening to her.

At first, she thought he must have been joking. He was surely winding her up? But when she saw how shaken her husband was, and how unlike Anthony he was being, she realised he was telling the truth.

Initially, she laughed, more out of shock than anything else. She had spent the whole week getting her head around the idea of staying with Anthony, and throwing every part of herself into their relationship at last, making it work for the best. In her mind, they would have lived a content, quiet life, perhaps with a bit more travel and the opportunity to explore new places together in a way they hadn't done in the past.

Once Anthony had told her about what took place, including the build-up and the excitement that caused him to do it, it wasn't jealously that she felt. It was disappointment that she herself hadn't discovered that side of him, after so many years of marriage together. There was also part of her that felt reinvigorated by the prospect that Anthony actually had that side to him. She knew only too well that life has a peculiar way of throwing in the most unexpected curve balls from time to time, and this had been the most unexpected of the lot.

After what had been an awkward conversation, Lucinda had suggested that perhaps the best course of action was to get home to Ferryman's Cottage and work out what they wanted to do next. Lucinda hadn't fully digested the situation, and her initial instinct was that they could probably find a way to make it work once back at home. But it was only once their bags were packed and the driver was waiting to take them to the airport that

Anthony had dropped the real bombshell. He didn't want to return home.

He announced to Lucinda that the experience, rather than leaving him feeling appalled and embarrassed, had, in fact, made him feel liberated, and more importantly, for the first time in his life, wanted. Instead, he was going to fly back to Northern California with Noelle, who lived in the small town of Mendocino on the edge of the Van Damme State Park, about three hours north of San Francisco. He said he had wanted "to give it a go" and explained that every aspect of his life had been predictable until this moment. It was time to take some risks.

Shocked, Lucinda replied, more out of vengeance than anything else, 'Anthony, if you had only been slightly less predictable over the last twenty-two years then we wouldn't have found ourselves in this bloody mess in the first place!' But as the words came out of her mouth, she knew the words would only serve to affirm his decision.

With that, Lucinda marched past him with her bag and climbed into the waiting taxi, without looking back. As she drove out of the gates, she saw Noelle, standing conspicuously by the reception desk with her bags packed at her feet.

On the flight home, Lucinda tried to make sense of the situation over several double gin and tonics. Her emotions wavered from bewilderment to anger, but soon all feelings of rage subsided, and a melancholic sadness overwhelmed her.

Perhaps it was the gin, but the reality dawned on her that Anthony, her husband of twenty-two years, had gone.

A feeling of loneliness gripped every part of her body, and the empty seat next to her only caused her more pain. Tears began to roll down her face.

*

After a hideous journey and a few days back at Ferryman's Cottage, Lucinda tried to work out what on earth would happen next with her life. Eventually, she decided to revert to her original plan before Christmas, as if she had been the one who left Anthony, not the other way around. She had called Pauline, and a week later her trip to South Africa had been arranged. She planned to go for an initial four months, then return home for Sophie's wedding.

Lucinda had spent many evenings looking out over the Franschhoek Valley, trying to comprehend what had happened, and what Anthony's thought process must have been. She considered every option, playing them through in her mind each evening before going to sleep. Sometimes she wondered whether she would ever hear from him again.

The sheer suddenness of the move, and self-destruction of the existence he had built up over his entire life, was just not in her husband's character. She didn't need to be a psychologist to recognise that Anthony's life had been suppressed his entire existence. She also recognised that she had been responsible for much of that behaviour, and rather than managing their relationship with only the small amount of care and maintenance that Anthony required, she knew she had allowed the relationship to corrode.

She had gone to South Africa not just for the adventure, but also to take time for herself to work out how she wanted to spend the rest of her life. When she arrived, she was open-minded about her options and hadn't ruled out staying for longer, perhaps even indefinitely. But as comfortable as life was out there in the Western Cape of South Africa, and the friends she had made over the last four months, she knew it was not *her* place. She missed nattering with her friends and the view from her kitchen window, overlooking the church. She missed Sophie and Jack most of all, and their weekend visits to the house. Hell, she even missed the grumpy shopkeeper at her local Londis! And she missed Anthony, particularly his presence, if not always his conversation.

Although she didn't admit as much, Lucinda had felt ready, and in need, to be in touch with Anthony. Any feelings of anger she'd had towards him were now outweighed by concern. He hadn't made any attempt to justify his actions to anyone, only apologising profusely to both Sophie and Jack, explaining he needed to explore certain things in life. Lucinda had seen many relationships between couples their age become irreparably damaged, leaving a trail of grief, misery and destruction for themselves and those closest to them. But she just couldn't believe that their marriage would end like that.

But Lucinda also couldn't bring herself to reach out to Anthony; nor did she know exactly where he was. There had been no attempt to retrieve any of his belongings from the house, which comforted her somewhat.

The most likely outcome, surely, would be that he would wake up one day and wonder what on earth he was doing living with a Californian hippy nymphomaniac. Anthony was not a hippy. He was a man who liked walks in the countryside, doing DIY in the garden and watching Sunday afternoon television with a decent bottle of Chianti. He was, after all, predictable.

Having not exchanged a word since the morning of their departure in Mexico, Lucinda finally woke up to find an email from her estranged husband.

My Dear Lucinda,

How strange it has been these last few months. Not a word exchanged between us since I last saw you, after twenty-two years of marriage.

Of course, I recognise we had our blips during that time, and I was not always there to support you as I know a companion should have been. But the truth is, Lucinda, I love you and have nothing but the highest admiration for you. More now than ever.

The last four months have been a strange whirlwind and mix of emotion, the like of which I could not have previously comprehended. I have been living with Noelle, in her wooden house, in a small and rather hippy community. We grow our own food and spend a lot of time in the nearby redwood trees doing group forest bathing exercises. Three evenings a week I volunteer in a local library, which hosts book clubs. I think it has certainly been enlightening but, if truth be told, I think I am now sufficiently enlightened and am probably rather better suited to life in England.

More importantly, I miss you, Lucinda. I miss the life we had together. Dare I say, but I miss the predictability of it too. I think it was Horace Walpole who once said: 'When people will not weed their own minds, they are apt to be overrun by nettles.' If nothing else, this time in Northern California has enabled me to weed my mind. I know with every fibre of my body that I would like to return home and make a fresh start with you. Clearly, we are not as young as we once were, but I would still hope there are plenty of miles left in the tank. I want to make the most of those miles with you; not like it was before, but with spontaneity, travel (though perhaps not Tulum?) and learning.

Sophie wrote to me last week about her wedding, expressing her desire for me to still walk her down the aisle; I cannot tell you how much that means to me after everything I have put you all through these last few months. That said, I fully understand if you would rather I was not there. I told her I would speak with you first. What do you think?

I hear from Sophie you're now with Pauline and Greg on the wine farm in South Africa. I know you had been wanting to visit them for a long time, so delighted to hear you've finally done so.

Funny thing life and the twists and turns it throws at us, isn't it?

I hope to hear back from you soon.

With my love and deepest apologies,
Anthony

Reading the email, Lucinda could identify many of Anthony's familiarities, but there was a certain freshness to his tone, and an outlook which she had not seen before. She had grown to develop a newfound respect for her estranged husband.

Anthony had raised Sophie, and he was the closest thing she had to a father. After his email, there had been a great deal of correspondence back and forth between Sophie, Lucinda and Jack, debating whether they wanted him at the wedding at all, let alone to give him the honour of walking the bride down the aisle. Finally, they reached the consensus that he should be there. Sophie was pretty much in denial about the fact that Anthony had left, putting his absence down to an extended holiday in her mind. And Jack had continued to behave unexpectedly sweetly towards his mother, in a way he perhaps hadn't before.

Perhaps it was the amount of South African wine that Lucinda had drunk over the last four months that allowed her to adopt a far more pragmatic and optimistic approach to life. She knew that her relationship with Anthony wasn't irreparably broken, but it needed some serious maintenance.

That evening, she drafted a number of replies to Anthony's email, ranging from long explanations of her feelings and critiques of their relationship together, to more aloof summaries, written more in spite than with any concerted effort to reach harmony. Having see-sawed back and forth in her tone, in the end she opted only to respond with:

We are all looking forward to seeing you, very much.
Lucinda x

Acknowledgements

We live in a world more confused and polarised than ever, yet there has never been a better time to be alive. I fear sometimes we have forgotten how to enjoy life and fail to focus enough on what matters, and what does not. How extraordinary it is that we exist at all. This book was written with the single objective of trying to make people smile, at least a little more.

I have relied on the help of a few supportive friends who, not only smile a lot themselves but have been invaluable in the development of this story. In particular, I must thank Charlotte, Rosie and Katy, whose early feedback and helpful notes have been enormously helpful and much appreciated.

Also to Anna, who did everything she could to make the book more readable by providing encouragement and criticism in equal measure. You make me smile everyday, thank you.

And finally, and possibly most importantly, to the dreadlocked woman on Tulum beach who fed me the chocolate cake. I have no idea who you are, but I hold you responsible for the story that unfolded! Thank you.